AF484912

Drawn from Life

RIFT ZONE

and other stories

a collection of short fiction by

Sarah P. Blanchard

RIFT ZONE

Content warning: Suicide, sexual assault, murder.

Cover design: Sarah P. Blanchard (photo by Makasanaphoto)

April 2026 Eagle Ridge Press
First Printing
ISBN 979-8-9996922-7-6 softcover
ISBN 979-8-9996922-9-0 ebook

For my parents Villa and Clifford,
always the best storytellers;
for Rich,
always beside me;
and for Phil,
who carries everything into the future.

CONTENTS

RIFT ZONE

and other stories

The Bus Driver

On Thursday, the last afternoon before spring break, Brandi Moorehead missed the afternoon bus.

She'd stayed a few minutes after class to talk with her seventh-grade English teacher about an assignment. Then the zipper failed on her cheap denim backpack, right after she'd shoved her old laptop in on top of three textbooks and her latest knitting project. By the time the janitor helped her seal the top with masking tape, it was three-thirty and she was alone in the hallway.

She hurried down the concrete steps to the bus pickup point, but she was too late. The parking lot was empty, all the buses gone.

How could the afternoon driver—that orange-haired woman with the screechy voice—leave without her?

George, her morning bus driver, the man she was secretly in love with, wouldn't have left her behind.

Brandi pulled out her phone and stared at the blank screen. It was an old flip phone with an unreliable battery, and she'd forgotten to charge it the night before.

Who could she call, anyway? Her mom's shift at McDonald's wasn't over until seven and Brandi wasn't supposed to call her at work unless it was an emergency.

She absolutely would not call Uncle Eddie, not even if her phone was working. Not even if he could borrow a car from one of his buddies. Not even if he was sober.

She decided to go home on foot. She'd done this once before, a month earlier, when she'd stayed late to work on her science fair project. That day, her mom had arranged to leave work early and pick her up halfway at a gas station. Brandi had enjoyed the walk.

Today, she'd walk the whole eight miles. It would take about three hours, maybe less. If she got a blister, she'd stop at the gas station, borrow a phone, and wait there until her mom got off work. But she didn't expect blisters. She was wearing her best leather boots, the red-laced LL Beans she'd scored at Goodwill.

Pleased with her plan, she quickly braided back her long black hair and shrugged into her taped-up backpack.

The first hour went well. The sun was warm on her shoulders, and she found a good rhythm. She was in a familiar part of town with small tidy homes, many bordered by brilliant azalea bushes in full bloom. She passed a convenience store that advertised firewood, bait worms, and lottery tickets. On the sidewalks, people walked dogs and pushed baby strollers.

One hour in, she passed the gas station where she'd met her home the time before. Brandi glanced at the clock in the store and kept going, pleased to see she was making good time. If she ignored the dog-walkers and baby strollers, she could pretend she was hiking the Appalachian Trail. Her math teacher had done the whole Trail last year, through-hiking from Georgia to Maine. What a great adventure that must have been, sleeping in a tent like an old-time explorer and carrying everything you needed to survive in the mountains.

She wondered if George liked to hike. She didn't know much about him—didn't know *anything* about him, really—but he looked like he'd enjoy hiking. She'd watched him closely every morning from her seat on the big yellow bus—the same seat every day, fourth row, right side, on the aisle, where she could see his face in the rearview mirror. She'd memorized every handsome feature: short dark hair, a neatly sculpted beard, and steel-rimmed glasses that made him look especially sensitive and intelligent. His skin was a medium warm brown with darker freckles over his cheeks and he appeared to be in his mid-twenties, mature but not too old for a serious young woman like herself.

For the past three months, George had occupied all of Brandi's dreams and daydreams. This was her deepest secret, and she'd absolutely die of shame if he ever found out.

It was easy to keep secrets if you didn't try to make friends. When Brandi and her mom had first moved into Uncle Eddie's house right after Christmas, Brandi tried to figure out the social complexities at her new school. An only child who'd always been homeschooled, she'd been overwhelmed by the hierarchies and social intrigues of a small-town Appalachian middle school where all the other kids had been forging alliances and nursing grudges since nursery school.

She'd been taunted, then ignored, for her thrift shop clothes, her old phone and even older laptop. She had no money for music or makeup and no interest in boys her age. In school, she often thought of herself as a ghost. Even the teachers occasionally forgot her name.

Despite what her classmates thought of her—if they thought of her at all—Brandi paid close attention to her appearance. She wanted George to see her as she really was: mature, serious, competent. Not a clueless, awkward thirteen-year-old whose widowed mother was barely keeping a roof over their heads.

Every little thing mattered as Brandi prepared for her bus ride each morning. As soon as the headlights of the yellow bus appeared in the pre-dawn darkness beneath a morning star, Venus or Jupiter or sometimes Saturn, she centered her old denim backpack precisely on her back and arranged her long hair in a smooth black curtain over her shoulders. Then she stood very casually, waiting for the bus to whoosh to a stop and the doors to fold open. She knew exactly how to grasp the cold metal handrail with her left hand and climb gracefully up the steep steps without sprawling. On the top step, she always paused, heart thumping, to gaze down into George's warm brown eyes.

"Morning." He had a lovely baritone voice and he always smiled at her. That's when her carefully choreographed script fell apart. Too nervous to speak, she'd redden and duck forward so her hair swung over her face. Then she'd stumble down the aisle, furious with embarrassment.

A few minutes later, when the flush had faded and her pulse quit racing, she'd push her hair back and spend the rest of the morning bus ride with her eyes glued to George's face in the rearview mirror. Sometimes he stared back, holding her gaze for a few seconds and smiling a little, just with his eyes, before turning his attention back to the road.

If she were older, she could ask him to teach her to drive. He drove the bus very carefully and she knew he'd be good in a crisis. If they were in an accident—if the bus skidded on ice and flipped over or a big truck sideswiped them into a ditch—George would know exactly how to get everyone out safely. He'd be her hero.

And they could do things together, but not stupid things like parties or dancing. Canoeing and fishing, or horseback riding, like she used to do with her dad. Maybe they could even hike part of the Appalachian Trail.

Where she walked now was definitely not the Appalachian Trail. The tidy residential neighborhood with its azaleas, sidewalks, and strollers had disappeared. Now she was dodging mud, potholes, and broken glass on broken pavement. Houses in this part of town weren't much more than shacks, small and fragile-looking, with thistles and pokeweed growing in trash-strewn yards. She saw house trailers with broken windows, boarded-up sheds, and skeletons of old cars sitting on blocks or rusting quietly into the weeds. She'd never liked the bus ride through this part of town and now she was seeing it up close and ugly. She quickened her pace.

She heard the snarl before she saw the dog, a big rawboned hound that lunged from beneath a tangle of blackberries. She jerked aside and felt her backpack lurch, tipping her sideways. As she grabbed a mailbox to stay upright, she heard a loud *rip* and a textbook thumped to the ground beside her.

The dog hurled itself at her, but landed a few yards short when it hit the end of its chain, which was fastened to the axle of an old pickup. Her pulse still pounding, Brandi scooped up her fallen math book and hurried to the far side of the road. As she lowered her backpack to the dirt, a side seam split wide, spilling out pens and notebooks. Her repair job had failed.

Muttering invectives and fighting tears, she stuffed everything back in, wrapped her arms around it, and began walking. But it was awkward and she knew she wouldn't get far, clutching the heavy pack in front of her chest.

She stopped and hung it by its frayed straps on a chain link fence. Stupid, she thought, leaving the masking tape at school. She had her knitting wool, though. Maybe she could wrap lots of yarn around the bag to hold it together. Then she remembered her red bootlaces. Those would be stronger than yarn.

As she crouched to untie the laces, she heard footsteps. She paused, her pulse quickening again. Not a dog, a person. Or people.

"Hey there, little girl. You lost?" The voice was male, with a local drawl. Brandi stood, keeping a hand on her backpack.

Two Black men watched her from a few yards away. One slouched casually against a utility pole while the other, smaller and younger, stood uneasily by the edge of the road. They wore identical saggy jeans, black hoodies, dreads, and snarky grins.

Brandi's breathing steadied. They weren't as old as she'd thought. Teens trying to look menacing, boys rather than men. But still older and bigger than her.

She stared at the younger boy. "Jamar? I know you. You're in my homeroom. Well, sometimes you're there."

Jamar's thin smile slipped.

The older boy shot him a glance, grinning. "Dude, you know this hot babe? You in school with her?"

"Yeah," Jamar admitted. "Her name's Brandi. Brandi *Moore*-head." He recovered his smirk. "Not even half hot, though."

Brandi rolled her eyes like the other girls. "That's lame. Like no one's ever said my name *that* way before." She hoped she'd hit the right mix. Cool, unbothered but not disrespectful.

The older one drawled, "So, Bran-dee *Moore*-head. You look like you are lost and you maybe need us to help you. That is one sad-ass shitty bag you got there." He nodded at her backpack. "We'll get you a nice new one, real pretty. Put some bling on, fill it with good shit. Then we get some weight on you. Dress up that flat white-girl thang you call an ass. You gonna be real pretty." He shook his head slowly and added a mock frown. "It's gonna take work, though. And you gotta smile, girl. You got one serious bitch face going on there."

"I'm not lost," Brandi shot back. "Right now you're getting my very best smile, so call it what you want. I don't need any help, thank you." Did her voice tremble at the end? She fervently hoped not.

Jamar said, "Yeah, well, maybe you be okay, but that backpack didn't get the memo." He snort-laughed, delighted with his own wit.

She ignored Jamar and kept her eyes on the older one, considering options. Could she convince them she wasn't worth the trouble? Should she leave her backpack and run, or pitch a fit and scream? She was a fast runner, but she didn't want to abandon her laptop. She'd never practiced screaming, so she probably wasn't very good at that.

The older boy moved closer. She felt the back of her neck prickle as she eased a hand into her backpack. Where was her phone? The battery was dead, but he wouldn't know that.

As he reached for her arm, she swung one booted foot up hard and fast, aiming for his crotch but catching his kneecap. He cried out, twisting away.

"Fuck!" He brought up a fist and lunged forward.

"Asshole," she muttered. She slipped on loose gravel and went down on one knee but came up fast, her right hand gripping a thick aluminum knitting needle. The tip was pointed at his belly and her stance said she was ready for a knife fight.

The big boy growled at Jamar. "Fuckin idiot, get up here."

Jamar hesitated and Brandi was glad she hadn't untied her shoelaces. Maybe now was the right time to run.

"Hey! What's going on here?"

Brandi's would-be assailants turned to stare at a pickup truck coming toward them. And just like that, it was over. Both boys bolted across the road and faded into the weeds behind a boarded-up shed.

The pickup, dirty black where it wasn't rust-colored, rolled to a stop beside her. The driver leaned across the seat to peer at her through the open passenger window.

"Hey there," he said. "It's Brandi, right? You okay?"

Brandi blinked and stared back. Her stomach lurched. "George? How—?"

"I just finished my high school run, I'm heading home. You all right? What happened?"

"I'm okay. They were just hassling me a little." She reached up to pull her hair over her face, but it was still tied back in a braid.

Stupid, she thought. I can talk to bullies but not my bus driver.

"That was a pretty good kick you threw." He left the engine running and got out, looking up and down the street before he joined her by the chain link fence. He was wearing the same clothes she'd seen him in at six that morning. Denim vest, old jeans, and a green flannel shirt. He nodded at the knitting needle in her hand. "That's an interesting choice of weapon, Miz Morehead."

"You know my name?" She slid the knitting needle into her backpack. "I hate my name."

"Yeah. Us drivers are supposed to know everyone. Who you are, where you live. Where's your ride?"

"I missed the bus," she admitted, "so I'm walking. I'd be almost home if this stupid backpack wasn't falling apart." Her eyes threatened to tear up, so she rubbed a hand over her face.

"Hey, it's okay. They're not coming back. They know I saw them. Where's your phone? You need me to call someone? What about your mom?"

"Mom's working until seven. There's no one else."

"No neighbors? What about the Everetts? They live near you. I'd call an Uber for you, but I don't think they'll come out here."

Brandi shook her head. "We don't know the Everetts." She added, "Maybe *you* could give me a ride? You can pretend you're an Uber." Never having lived where there were Ubers, she wasn't sure how it worked.

George folded his arms and leaned against the hood of his truck. He scanned the street, frowning. "Sorry, I'm not an Uber driver. With this truck? And here's this other thing. We can't have a big ol' Black man, that's me, taking a little White girl, that's you, for a ride in his truck. What do you think that looks like? I can't take that chance."

She was stung. He'd called her "little." Was that how he saw her?

Then she heard the rest of what he'd said. "That's ridiculous. You're helping me. There's nothing wrong about that."

"Uh-huh." He scratched the back of his head. "I could call the police for you. They'd give you a ride home."

"No, no police!" she insisted. Police would scare Eddie. He'd disappear and they'd be evicted because Mom couldn't pay the rent on her own. So no, no police. But she couldn't say all that to George.

He glanced around again and sighed. "Get in, I'll drive you."

Not quite believing it, she hauled the creaky passenger door open before he changed his mind. Set her broken backpack on the seat and climbed in. The truck started rolling while she was still fumbling with the seatbelt.

The mixture of delight and relief brought courage. "I'm not White," she volunteered. "Well, not all of me. My birth daddy is—was—half Paiute. We lived on a ranch on the Snake River. That's in Idaho." She was babbling but didn't care.

He raised an eyebrow. "A real ranch, like riding horses and branding cattle?"

"We had horses and my dad ran some cattle. Mostly it was a dude ranch for tourists who wanted an 'authentic western experience.'" She air-quoted the phrase. "Dad was the wrangler and Mom cooked. I saddled horses and helped teach the dudes how to ride. Took the kids fishing sometimes."

He slowed for a turn, then resumed his sedate pace, five miles under the speed limit. "Sounds like a great life. How'd you end up here?"

Brandi hesitated, planning what to say and what to leave out. "Last October, my dad died in a tractor accident." She swallowed around the lump in her throat. "The people who owned the ranch had to hire someone else to run it. When the new people came, we had to move out. Mom and me."

"You loved your dad." A statement, not a question.

"Yeah. He was the best."

"Then what happened?"

Her voice steadied. "Uncle Eddie said Mom and I could come here and live with him. Mom got a job at McDonalds." She bit her lip. She shouldn't have mentioned Eddie.

George's brow furrowed. "Who's Uncle Eddie?"

"He's Mom's third cousin or something like that. They're related but not real close. It's his house—well, he rents it. He told me to call him Uncle Eddie."

"He's working, too? He couldn't come pick you up?"

She was silent for a moment. "He doesn't work. He got PTSD from Iraq and now he gets checks from the government. He drinks a lot and Mom says don't bother him, just stay out of his way when he gets bad."

George flicked a quick look at her. "What's that mean, when he gets bad? And how often is that?"

She'd started the story and couldn't stop now. "He gets angry sometimes and wakes up yelling. He goes out most nights to a bar and his buddies bring him back around midnight. He sleeps downstairs. Mom and I have rooms upstairs. Mom made a rule, his buddies can't come in the house unless she's there. They're not so bad. I think they take care of him."

"So you're not supposed to bother Eddie. Does he bother you?"

She knew what he was asking. "Only twice," she said slowly. "Once I woke up and he was in my room, standing over me. Then Mom came home and that scared him away. I told Mom and the next day we got locks for our bedroom doors. The other time was in the daytime. I was in the kitchen. He came up behind me and I told him he was too close. When he didn't back away, I grabbed a knife and cut his arm. Then I ran outside. I carry a knife when I'm home and I keep my door locked if Mom's not there. I think," she added, "Eddie's a little afraid of me."

"But you can't carry a knife back and forth to school."

"I keep it hidden in the woods. And I have my knitting needles. I'm making a scarf."

"You can get those into school?"

"They're plastic."

"You are just one surprise after another." He smiled briefly before the worried look returned. "Seriously, you and your mom need to talk with social services about Eddie. You are not in a good situation, Brandi."

"No! If we can't stay with Eddie, we'll have to live in our car. We don't have enough money to get an apartment. Mom says it's all about circumstances. When our circumstances improve, we'll find a better place to live." Maybe she was telling him too much, but it felt good to talk.

She thought of something else. "Eddie yells at my mom sometimes, but he's never hit her. She told him she carries."

"A pistol."

"Yeah."

"Here," Brandi said suddenly. "Let me out here, please. I can walk the rest."

They'd reached the turn for her road. The sun was low in the sky, and she realized that without George's help, she wouldn't have made it home before dark.

He pulled over, set the truck's parking brake, and let it idle.

"And does your mom carry?" George asked.

Brandi looked away. "I'm not supposed to tell anyone. Or call the police. Mom says we can solve our own problems."

"I believe you can." He smiled. "Hey, maybe I *should* get a job with Uber. Think anyone would want to ride in this old truck?"

Brandi looked down. She could see pavement and gravel through holes in the floor. "Sure. I definitely would. I *do* ride with you. Every day on the bus." She blushed a little.

George draped both hands over the top of the steering wheel. "Why do you hate your name?"

"Moorehead was my bio dad's name. The half-Paiute guy, I don't remember him. Mom said he was real mean to her. She kicked him out when I was about a year old. She met my stepdad when I was two. His name is—was—Alex Carter. Mom wanted to get a divorce from the other guy, but she couldn't track him down so she never got it and she couldn't get married again. We lived with my stepdad, my real dad, for ten years but then he died. It's real hard on her." She was starting to choke up again, so she grimaced instead. "My name—Brandi Moorehead—it sounds like a porn star."

"Yeah, I can see where the kids would have fun with that. What name would you like?"

"Something that isn't cute, that doesn't sound like a baby's nickname. That doesn't end in an 'ee' sound. I like

Harper, like Harper Lee. Or Erin, like Erin Brockovich. Erin Carter, how does that sound?"

"I think Erin Carter sounds great," George said. "Hey, you know the Randolph farm down by the river? If you give them a hand with the livestock, I bet they'd let you ride one of their horses. Just tell Miz Randolph that George Kulikowski sent you."

"Who—? That's your name?"

He laughed. "Yeah. my daddy's daddy was Polish, a refugee in World War Two. You're part Paiute, I'm part Polish. So you never know, right?" His eyes crinkled at the corners, and she realized he was older than she'd thought.

"Now go, before someone comes and we have to answer questions." He held out his hand and she shook it firmly. She was surprised not to feel thrilled by his touch. It felt instead like the warm handshake of a friend.

"Thank you, George Kulikowski," she said politely. She gathered the contents of her backpack and scrambled out of the truck, then butted the heavy door closed with her hip.

"Goodbye, Erin Carter," George said. "I believe you'll do just fine."

The truck pulled away and she waited a moment, watching it disappear around a bend in the road. She walked home in the early evening dusk, feeling buoyant and knowing her face was stretched into a big goofy smile. If she hadn't had both arms wrapped around the backpack, she'd have skipped along like a little kid.

On Saturday, Brandi spent most of the day in the woods, exploring a new trail that she thought might be a shortcut to the Randolph farm and thinking about cows and horses.

At dinnertime, she saw that Eddie's biker jacket, fake cowboy boots, and greasy duffel bag were missing from the hallway.

"Where's Eddie?" she asked.

Her mom shrugged. "I don't know. Someone from the sheriff's office called, wanting to talk to him. I said he was out, I'd have him call them back. When he came home with a couple of friends, he just grabbed all his stuff and took off. He didn't say where he was going, just that something came up and he needed to move on."

"But what about us? Can we stay here?"

"We're fine. Eddie's landlord says you and I can stay on if we can manage the rent. April's paid for and I'll figure something out before May. If you ever see that S.O.B. again, tell me, okay?"

They celebrated by going out for Chinese. Brandi found a sturdy new backpack at Goodwill.

A few days later, their new housemate moved in, a friend of a friend of the manager at McDonalds, an older woman who'd relocated from Puerto Rico after losing her home in a hurricane. She needed a cheap place to live with her two rescue dogs, a shy Chihuahua and an arthritic old pit bull.

Their new housemate insisted that Eddie's old downstairs room would be perfect for her and the dogs once she'd hung the door back on its hinges and disinfected everything.

The Sunday before she went back to school, Brandi finished knitting a navy wool scarf. She wrapped it carefully in a brown paper bag, wrote "George K" on the outside, and tucked it into her new backpack. Spring was absolutely not the right time to give anyone a wool scarf, but it was all she had to give him.

On Monday morning, she waited for the school bus with the bag in one hand. She'd smile and say "Hi, good morning," and "This is for you." She wouldn't be nervous. Instead, she was thinking about how they could be friends. She could maybe meet him in a coffee shop some Saturday afternoon and chat the way friends do. She'd have to research coffee shops first and figure out what a latte was.

But George wasn't there. The orange-haired screechy woman was in George's seat.

"Where's George!?" She was close to tears.

The woman shrugged. "Find your seat, girl. We're running late already."

That afternoon, she found an envelope wedged under the arm of the red flag on their mailbox. It was addressed to Erin Carter and her heart rose into her throat even as she opened it.

Dear Erin, I know you didn't want things stirred up, but I made a couple of phone calls and I think circumstances will get better for you and your Mom. Hang in there and take care of each other. I was worried about you before, but not so much now.

I'm starting a new job. I'll miss seeing your face in the rearview mirror every morning.

All my best, George Kulikowski (the Polish guy)

She carried the scarf at the bottom of her backpack for a while, just in case she saw him somewhere. After a month, she tucked it away in the back of her closet, still wrapped in the brown paper bag with his name on it. His note, carefully folded, remained in the keepsake box on her dresser for a much longer time.

That summer Erin Carter and her mom hiked fifty-three miles of the Appalachian Trail, carrying on their backs everything they needed to survive in the wilderness.

A Good Voice for Horses

Jennie Holstrom propped her cane against a post and held the top rail of the paddock fence with stiff hands. She shifted her weight a little to the left, easing the ache in her bad hip. Eight in the morning came earlier now than it used to. She should have taken her pain meds an hour ago, but it was more important to get her old horse fed and settled into his retirement home.

She glanced at the small, quiet boy peering through the fence a dozen feet away.

Jennie jerked her chin at the old horse. "That old fella doesn't look like much, does he? That's Harry. He's so sway-backed and shaggy, he couldn't even get a job now as a poor man's scarecrow. But he was pretty famous in his day, a world-class show jumper. Even had his own fan club."

She narrowed her eyes at the boy. "You don't have any idea what I'm talking about, do you?"

The solemn-faced kid shook his head slowly but didn't take his eyes off the tall pinto gelding. He looked eight or maybe nine. Maybe younger. Jennie wasn't good at guessing kids' ages, not having had any of her own.

She didn't know the boy's name, but she thought she'd seen him waiting for the yellow school bus at the end of the new neighbors' driveway. On this early autumn Sunday, he'd simply materialized beside her as she watched Harry nibble grass in his paddock.

The old horse wandered beneath a large oak tree, his mottled coat fitting nicely into the patches of sun and shadow. A small donkey watched from the next paddock, twitching her thin tail and swiveling her long, furry ears.

"Harry's full name is Houdini's Apprentice," Jennie continued. "He was a champion and he won big prizes. Blue ribbons, trophies, lots of money. Harry could jump six feet high and twenty feet wide. He traveled all over the world, he was shortlisted for the Pan Am Games. That's almost like the Olympics. You've seen the Olympics, on TV maybe?"

The boy kept his dark, serious eyes on Harry. He nodded again, just a little.

She tried again. "Do you like horses?"

A more vigorous nod.

"Harry's a pinto. In England, they call that color a piebald, but here it's just a black-and-white pinto. Kind of funny looking, isn't he, with one black ear and one white ear? That big white face, and those blue eyes. After Harry's settled in, you can give him an apple. Would you like to help me take care of him? No riding, though. He's twenty-eight, too old. That's like eighty-five for a human."

Crouching forward on the toes of dirty sneakers, the boy leaned into the gap between the top and middle rails of the fence, pushed his head and shoulders through.

He'll topple into the paddock, Jennie thought, *if he tips forward any farther. And he hasn't said a single word. Is he hard of hearing, or just shy? Or maybe a little, what do they call it, developmentally different?*

"Here," she said sharply, "get back on *this* side of the fence! Before you fall in and scare Harry." She didn't mean to be harsh, but she was worried the boy might not understand. "Don't go climbing on the fence, or the gates, either. This old place, something's likely to break. Then you'll get hurt and your mother will come over here and give me hell."

The boy scrambled back from the fence and whipped around to face her. Black hair flopped over his forehead and his dark eyes welled with tears. He spun away, sprinted across the yard, and disappeared into the pine woods beyond her house.

"Hey," Jennie called. "I'm sorry! I didn't mean to frighten you. What's your name?" Too late, he was gone.

She felt bad about scaring the boy. He reminded her of a startled colt, spooked by loud voices and quick movements. Just the way Harry had been when he'd first arrived here on her farm as a half-wild yearling, nearly three decades ago.

Jennie had been in her late thirties then, working hard to create a successful training business. She'd coached young riders and trained young horses, mostly for the amateur circuit. The mild climate in North Carolina's sandhills served her well and allowed her to do what she loved for thirty years. How many people get to say that about their life?

Harry had been an accidental acquisition, a feral colt she'd reluctantly accepted in trade for an unpaid board bill. The result of someone's what-were-they-thinking backyard breeding, he arrived with unknown parentage and a deep suspicion of humans. He was the most challenging horse she ever owned. But he also displayed a natural athleticism and quick, catlike reflexes. By the time he was three years old, he'd grown to seventeen hands and was turning heads—and not just because of his unusual coloring. He could leap every fence on her farm. Jennie knew that anyone who could gain Harry's trust would have a very talented jumper.

It had taken her six months of groundwork and another six months of slow trail rides to get his basic training sorted out. Harry was hyper-sensitive, a highly reactive horse who took offense at the slightest mistake. Not an amateur's ride, not a steady-eddy for the hunt field, and definitely not the best horse for a timid or heavy-handed rider.

But oh, how he could jump! Harry's ability to jump tall obstacles quickly outstripped Jennie's ability to ride him over tall obstacles, so she'd offered him to a young man with the skills and patience to develop his natural ability. Then the flashy pinto with the blue eyes became a show-ring phenomenon. Fans took selfies with Harry and brought him buckets of carrots at every show. Harry competed in Europe, Australia, South America.

When he could no longer jump the huge fences, Harry became the much-loved partner at lower levels for his rider's younger sister, and then a younger brother. Through all those years, Jennie followed his career closely.

Now Harry had come home. This was her deal with the family who owned him: When Harry grew old and tired, he would come back to Jennie. She was getting old, too. Now in her late sixties, she hadn't ridden in three years. Not since the car accident that broke her ankle and messed up her hip. After the accident, she'd sold most of the farm, keeping only a few acres, a small barn, and Poppy the donkey for companionship.

Then she waited for Harry.

He'd spent a few months out to pasture at his owners' farm but, after a few months with no adoring fans and no job, his appetite had flagged and he began losing weight. Jennie told them she had a stall ready for him.

To be honest, she was also feeling a bit selfish. She wanted to have her time with Harry—a few months at least—so she could say a proper goodbye when he was ready to go.

Jennie pulled a carrot out of her jeans pocket and wiggled it in Harry's direction, hoping to catch his attention. But he ignored her, choosing instead to cock a hip and settle into a nap under the oak tree.

She stuck the carrot back in her pocket and retrieved her cane.

Maybe the boy would come back tomorrow, after school. It would be nice to have someone else around to help and talk to. She hoped she hadn't scared him off for good. Maybe he'd decided he didn't like horses, after all. That would be a shame.

The boy didn't wait until the next day. When Jennie walked to the barn for evening chores, she spotted him at the edge of the woods, standing very still beneath a pine tree.

"Hello again." She smiled and kept her voice friendly. "I'm sorry I yelled, earlier. I just didn't want you to get hurt. Would you like to help me feed Harry and Poppy?

Poppy's the donkey. However," she added as he came closer, "I do need to know your name. And how old you are."

He looked down and twisted a sneaker toe in the gravel. His mouth moved, but she couldn't hear anything.

"Sorry, can you speak up? I can't bend down so good." She leaned on her good leg, tucked a lock of gray hair behind an ear, and cocked her head in his direction.

He stepped closer and whispered. "Travis. Travis Williams." A pause. "I'm nine." He stepped back quickly and dropped his head again.

"Well, Travis, it's nice to meet you. My name is Jennie Holstrom. You can call me Miz Jennie, if you like. Or just Jennie, that works too."

She watched him try out her name, mouthing the words: "Miz Jennie."

"Okay, Travis. Would you like to help me feed Harry and Poppy? You can measure out the grain and carry some hay, okay?" She paused. "I'll need to talk with your parents before I let you do anything more than that. Your parents do know you're here, right? Where do you live?"

He pointed toward the woods.

"The red house on the corner or the gray one next over?"

Another whisper. "The gray one."

If she watched his face, she could make out what he was saying. She might have to brush up on her lip-reading skills.

They were in the feed room measuring grain when she heard a man's voice.

"Hello, anyone here? Travis, are you here?"

Travis set the grain scoop in the feed bin and ran into the barn aisle. He reappeared a moment later, tugging the hand of a square-built, dark-haired man.

Jennie smiled. "I'm Jennie Holstrom. You must be Travis's father. You look just like him."

"Jeff Williams, glad to meet you." He sounded tired. "Travis told you his name? That's good. He can be very shy. He's just started third grade. Being in a new school, meeting people—it's tough for him. I'm sorry he came over by himself. I told him I'd call first and maybe we'd come visit after I got off work—I manage the muffler shop and, yes, we work Sundays—but he couldn't wait. He saw the horse trailer arrive, early, while we were having breakfast. At noon, I heard all about Harry and Poppy."

So, Jennie thought, Travis can talk. And listen. He's not disabled or disadvantaged or whatever you call it. Just shy.

She said, "I'm happy to have Travis around. With your approval, of course. As long as he listens carefully and wants to work." She saw the boy smile. "We could do a trade, work for riding lessons. But not on Harry," she added quickly. "On Poppy, the donkey. Bareback."

Travis's smile broadened. Then he put on his serious face and picked up the grain scoop, awaiting instructions.

"Great, he'll love it." Jeff removed his watch and strapped it onto his son's thin wrist. "Be home by five-thirty, right?" Then, to Jennie, "Can I speak with you a moment, outside?"

"Sure." Jennie followed him to the end of the barn aisle.

Jeff shoved his hands in his front pockets and sighed. "I really appreciate this. You should know that my wife—" He paused and began again. "You need to know that Travis's mom is very sick. It's cancer, a brain tumor. We moved here to be close to the hospital. Marianne had surgery in July, and now she's got chemo every two weeks. Travis is our only kid, and he's taking it very hard. I've got this new job and—well, he's a really sweet kid, very quiet. He gets lost in the shuffle, sometimes. This will be good for him. So, thank you."

Such a burden, Jennie thought. *He's too young to carry all that. They are all too young.*

She touched his arm. "I'm so sorry. This must be hard for you. Whatever I can do, please, let me know. And I really can use Travis's help with the chores. But how can I get him to speak up? It's a safety issue. We need to communicate with the animals, and with each other."

"He'll get better about that as he gets to know you. He finds it easier to talk outdoors than when he's inside. That habit of his, the whispering? That's my fault." He rubbed his face with one hand. "Before the surgery, Marianne got these horrible headaches and I told Travis he needed to whisper because loud noises made her headaches worse. I told him he could help her get better by being very quiet."

"Ah," Jennie said. There was nothing to say, nothing that could take away the anguish in his face. All she could think was, *What if Travis wasn't perfectly quiet? What if he was quiet, and Marianne still didn't get better?*

Jeff turned to leave, then paused. "Can you send him home at five-thirty? He gets caught up and forgets the time. Any problems, please call my cell." He handed her a card with a phone number circled in red.

Back in the feed room with Travis, Jennie explained how to feed Harry and Poppy.

"Harry's old and missing a few teeth, so we'll add water to his grain and these chopped-up hay cubes to make it easy for him to eat. We'll make it mushy, like oatmeal. Poppy gets only a teeny handful of grain, plus one small flake of hay. Can you get that for her? When Harry's food is soaked, we'll open the stall doors and let them in."

Poppy ate quickly. Harry covered his muzzle with moist green slop but ate very little, and Jennie tried to hide her dismay. "He might have ulcers," she told Travis, "or a toothache. Horses can get those things, just like people. Or maybe he's just sad. At the big shows, there was always excitement. Lots of music, lots of people. Now his life is very quiet." She added, "My veterinarian is coming tomorrow morning, so we'll figure it out."

We'd better *figure it out,* she thought. *I don't want Travis to have someone else in his life get sick.*

She said, "Would you like to give him an apple? That's always been his favorite treat. Let's see if he has enough teeth left to chew a bit of apple."

Jennie produced a plastic bag of apple slices from her jacket pocket. She handed a piece to Travis and showed him how to hold it so his fingers wouldn't disappear inside Harry's mouth. Standing on tiptoes and reaching above the stall door, the small boy held his breath and offered the apple in a trembling hand. The big horse swiveled his ears forward and swung his head over the stall door. His nostrils fluttered as his wide pink and white muzzle explored the boy's hand. Then, with great care, Harry took the apple and chewed slowly.

Travis exhaled and grinned with delight. "He has whiskers! They tickle!" He spoke in a stage-whisper, still quiet but louder than anything he'd said earlier.

She handed Travis another piece of apple and a minute later Harry's harlequin head appeared again over the stall door. When Harry finished the second slice, he turned to his feed tub and began eating the green mush.

Jennie exhaled with relief. "Okay, time to go home," she told Travis. "Tomorrow, I'll show you how to put on a halter and how to lead a horse. Or a donkey. You can practice with Poppy, she's just your size."

Travis followed her outside. He whispered, "Thank you, Miz Jennie. See you tomorrow after school."

On Monday, Jennie learned from her vet that Harry appeared to be in reasonably good health.

"He's got some arthritis," Dr. Nickerson explained. "He's lost a few molars and the shaggy coat tells us he's got Cushing's. Metabolic syndrome. You've got him on a low-starch diet, so that's good. I'll run a blood panel, see if anything else turns up. And we'll treat him for ulcers. Otherwise, he seems okay. He's just, well, old."

"And depressed? Maybe he needs a job."

"We all need a reason to get up in the morning."

She stroked Harry's broad white forehead and nodded.

When Travis arrived that afternoon, Jennie was sitting in one of two lawn chairs she'd set up in the shade of the barn next to Harry's paddock. The boy sat in the second, his legs dangling. His face asked a question.

She said, "I'm watching Harry. Just watching. You can learn a lot by just watching."

Travis turned his gaze to the horse and settled into a position that copied Jennie's, leaning back a little with his hands relaxed on the arms of the chair and legs crossed at the ankles though his feet didn't reach the ground.

"So," she continued, "here's what I see. He looks a little more interested in everything today. He's walked over several times to say hi to Poppy. Did you notice yesterday, he didn't even swish his tail at the flies? Today his tail is working. He's had a good roll in the dirt to scratch his back. All those things tell me he's feeling better."

Travis nodded solemnly. Then, "Do horses get headaches?"

She had to lean in to hear him. Then she had to think for a moment because this seemed to be an important question.

"Maybe. If Harry bumped his head on something, I'm sure it would hurt. You learn to tell when a horse is in pain. They tense up around the nose and mouth, and the skin over their eyes gets wrinkly. They might hold their head to one side. But Harry's not telling me he's in pain. Maybe he's just a little stiff in the joints, like me."

"If he had a headache, we'd have to be real quiet, right? No music?"

"Right. But I don't think he has a headache. And he always seemed to enjoy the music at the shows."

"Maybe," Travis whispered, "Harry would like music."

"That's a good idea. You can help me set it up and choose some music. Something classical, or soft jazz. No reggae, no rap, and no heavy metal."

"What's that?"

"Stuff Harry wouldn't like. Or me."

Jennie told Travis about Dr. Nickerson's visit. The boy listened carefully.

"Overall," she said, "Harry is in pretty good shape for his age."

"So the doctor says Harry won't—" His voice faltered. "Die?"

"No, of course not—" Jennie corrected herself. "Well, not anytime soon, and not if I can help it. Harry is old so he needs special attention. That's why I had the vet come. To give him a checkup and help me figure out the best way to make him feel as good as possible."

"I'm glad you can fix Harry," he said. "I hope my mom's doctors can fix her. She gets a lot of headaches and she's really sick."

"Oh, honey," Jennie said gently. "I hope they can too." She stood awkwardly and turned toward the barn. "Time for your first lesson with Poppy."

Travis was a quick learner. He managed to halter the patient donkey on the second try. Then he went to work with a rubber curry comb, a soft brush, and a hoof pick. He practiced leading her around the paddock and had almost mastered tying a quick-release knot when Jennie called to him.

"I know Harry is really tall, and you're not, but if you can help me get his halter on and lead him into the stall, we can use the curry and brush on him, too. Get that mud off him."

Travis picked up Harry's halter and followed Jennie as she limped across the paddock. Travis was a little anxious. It was one thing to lean over the stall door and bravely feed Harry an apple, but something entirely different to walk up next to this huge animal and buckle a halter onto that gigantic head. But if Jennie told him he could do it, he would try his best.

Jennie rubbed Harry's dirty white forehead and hugged his thin neck. "Once," she explained, "I could call him in with a whistle. But I was in a car accident, and a couple of my teeth had to be replaced, and now I can't whistle. Can you whistle?"

"No." He'd never tried. "My dad used to but not now."

"Well, we can teach him to come to your voice, if you can call him loudly enough. He's got to hear you. And when we put his halter on, he needs to put his head down, so we use a voice command for that, too. Your voice needs to be steady and firm, but never angry or mean.

"Here," she explained. "Reach way up, put your hand high on his neck and say, 'Head down, Harry.' I taught him that, years ago. He's so tall, he has to put his head down to help us."

Travis tried. He reached up as high as he could but was only able to touch a black spot on Harry's shoulder, not way up his neck. He said, "Head down, Harry," but his voice was only a whisper. Harry didn't put his head down.

"Head down, Harry," Jennie said firmly. Her voice was quiet, but steady and firm.

She has a good voice for horses, Travis thought.

Harry hesitated, then lowered his head. Travis buckled the strap on Harry's halter. At least he remembered how to do that.

"You lead him now, and I'll follow," Jennie said.

Walking next to Harry's lowered head, the boy held the rope firmly. He wasn't exactly sure who was leading whom, but together they made their way slowly to the stall. Jennie limped behind.

"Well done," she said. "Now, I'll show you something new. Sometimes we have to ask a horse to step aside or back up. He takes up a lot of space in here, and sometimes we need him to move out of our way. Here's how."

Jennie planted her cane in the straw and stood at Harry's left side. She placed one hand on his broad ribcage and pushed gently. "Over, Harry," she said in her clear voice. Harry took two steps to the right. Then she stepped close to his front end, poked a finger firmly into the middle of his chest, and said, "Back, Harry, back." Harry stepped back two steps.

Travis was impressed, but his heart sank. He knew Harry wouldn't step over or back up for him, because Harry wouldn't be able to hear him. He couldn't summon that wonderful voice, those magical words that gave instructions to a horse.

He was glad that Jennie didn't ask him to practice speaking the commands, to move Harry sideways or backward. Instead, she handed him the rubber curry comb. "Let's get that mud off."

This he could do. He pushed the curry in big arcs over Harry's shoulder and saw the dried mud peel off. As he worked, the boy's mouth pursed into an experimental whistle-shape and he blew softly, producing a small, high sound. He saw one of Harry's ears flick in response.

Dust rose in shafts of late afternoon sunlight that slanted in through the open stall door. It's not just dirt, he thought. It's fairy dust, or magic glitter. He tried whistling again.

Harry curled his long neck sideways and swung his massive head gently toward Travis.

"Oh," the boy said softly. He dropped the curry comb and reached up with both arms, grasping the tangled mane and pulling himself tightly into the curve of the horse's shoulder.

"Don't move over, don't go back. Don't go anywhere," he whispered into Harry's warm neck. "Please, stay right here with me."

Rift Zone

The feral pigs have returned, pillagers from the Puna Forest Reserve. At two a.m. several are foraging outside June and Lani's bedroom window, snorting and grumbling. June hears their heavy bodies jostling against the house and each other, occasionally clattering over the lanai.

They churn the earth, rooting for papayas or guavas or avocados—or chicken feed, or a chicken—anything edible that's fallen outside the electric fence, the solar-powered perimeter that protects the gardens and henhouse with tensioned wires set at pig-snout height.

She lies on the mattress in the smoky orange gloom and thinks she should be grateful that it's the marauding pigs that woke her, not the Kilauea volcano. She can't hear the pigs at all when earthquakes shake the house, and lava explodes on the ridge.

Lani snores softly beside her. How can he possibly sleep? She calls his name softly, then with urgency.

"Lani. Lani! It's the pigs. You said to wake you if I hear the pigs. Lani, wake up! Pigs!"

She prods his shoulder. He grumbles and rolls away. She shakes him harder, and he snorts, piglike. Yawns, scratches his chin stubble, and sits up. Eighteen years together, but she's never figured out how he can sleep so deeply.

He never loses sleep like June does, worrying over the everyday things that leave her lying wide-eyed and panicky: too much rain, too little rain, never enough money, a broken-down truck, failed crops. How he can sleep now, with hot lava flowing over the roads and wild pigs roaming their yard, she has no idea.

Maybe it's the lack of kids. If they'd had children, it might be different. Then he'd have learned to sleep lightly and wake quickly. Or maybe not.

Lani stretches his lanky body and pivots off the mattress, fumbling for jeans and sneakers. He wrestles his tangled lion's mane into a rough twist and stuffs it under a grubby ball cap, then folds back the plastic tacked over the bedroom window. By the orange light of the volcano, he retrieves his .410 shotgun from the corner of the kitchen alcove.

June sits in half-lotus on the edge of the mattress and narrows her eyes against the smoky glow. She finger-combs dirty hair off her forehead and watches him load the gun, sliding a single shell into the chamber.

He loves this frontier existence. The elemental chaos of it, always skating on the edge of disaster. She doesn't know whether to laugh or cry at the absurdity of trying to defend their home from the pigs while there's a volcano erupting just beyond their doorstep.

She wants to scream it: *There's nothing left to defend.* Instead, she urges him silently: *Let's go. We should be packing, not shooting at hungry, displaced animals.*

He rests the gun barrel on the sill of the open window and swivels it slowly from side to side, sighting down its length and calculating where to spend his one precious shotgun shell to produce the greatest impact. Possibly kill one pig and send the rest back under the dead banana trees.

The shot won't be noticed. No one's living near enough anymore to hear it. A blast from a shotgun, the jet-engine roar from the lava flow, the crack of someone's propane tank exploding—it's all background noise, and who can tell the difference anyway?

Adam Tanaka's house is close, but he's nearly deaf and they haven't seen him for a few days. Last time they spoke, Adam said he was planning to go live with his niece, up the Hāmākua coast.

Before Lani can pull the trigger, the pigs throw up their heads, perhaps catching a scent of something more enticing. They blunder away, heading deeper into the 'ōhi'a forest behind Adam's place.

June shivers a little. The pigs are aggressive, unafraid of humans. They roam everywhere, even in good times. They destroy crops, dig up the land, and eat almost anything, including the carcasses of their own kind. She hates the pigs but she also hates seeing anything killed.

She feels a quick flicker of sympathy, an understanding of their desperation. They, too, are just trying to survive in this blasted land.

Lani exhales and straightens up. Thumbs the safety on and props the shotgun back in its corner.

"They stay gone now, but maybe they be back." He slips often these days into the local pidgin. "You sleep, I stay watch. Maybe I get 'em, by 'n by. Maybe not."

He gives her an apologetic smile and June thinks of the local phrase that first perplexed and then irritated her when she'd arrived on the Big Island nearly two decades earlier. *If can, can. If no can, no can.* She now knows that it's just another version of *que será, será.* What will be, will be. Or, *Hey, it ain't up to me,* which was another of Lani's annoying sayings.

"I need water. You wan' some?"

"Sure. Mahalo." She stretches out on their mattress again but knows she won't sleep. The pigs are gone and now she hears the thrum of a low-flying helicopter, heading east to track the lava flow. Another flyover by Civil Defense or the Hawaiian Volcano Observatory or the National Guard. Maybe all three.

Their home is only a few miles from the Pacific, but the night breezes don't smell like ocean anymore. The wind carries only a heavy, rank odor of sulfur and burned things, forests and homes and livestock.

Electricity is out, the overhead fan is motionless. With no good light to read by, all June can do at night is lie awake and worry and sometimes hope. She hopes the lava stops. Hopes they can agree about where to go and what to do, preferably before they run out of food, water, and fuel.

When she'd first arrived on the Big Island, the idea of living in this wild, fertile land had thrilled her. Growing up restless in a drab Connecticut city, she'd always yearned for a more vital life, close to the earth where she could grow her own food. At the end of her freshman year at a nondescript state college, she'd signed up for an exchange program at the University of Hawai'i. Not at the big Mānoa campus on Oahu, but in Hilo, a much smaller school on a much bigger island at the edge of vast rainforests and ranchlands.

In her first week at UH-Hilo, June Chamblee met Lani Shipman, a many-generations local boy, a college dropout with an easy laugh who worked at the local farm store, stacking pallets of hay and cattle feed. On their first date, they picked opihi limpets from the rocks at Kapoho tidepools and rode the surf at Honoli'i. She didn't need to finish college, Lani said. He'd teach her everything she needed to know about tropical farming and homesteading.

June's parents visited once, just after she'd dropped out of college. Worry framed all their questions: *What about finishing your degree? What about a career or at least a job with benefits? And why are you living next to an active volcano?*

Lani laughed off their concerns, leaving June to explain. The climate is gentle. You can grow or catch or create almost everything you need if you remember to respect the a'ina. The land.

And the volcano? Kilauea has been erupting gradually, quietly, since 1983. It's twenty miles away in Volcanoes National Park. Let's go see it, we'll hike the old craters and visit the sulfur banks. Watch the lava, oozing slowly toward the sea.

June's parents went home to Connecticut without seeing sulfur banks or lava fields. Over the years they'd faithfully sent cards and money on birthdays and holidays, but they never returned.

June never quite found the time to leave the farm long enough to visit them, seven thousand miles away on the mainland.

Lani's boundless confidence and love for the land drew her into an exciting new life. They swam in a dozen waterfalls, camped beneath the cliffs in Waipi'o Valley. On the slopes of Mauna Kea, she watched meteors flash through the darkest skies she'd ever seen.

We should buy one homestead lot in Puna district, Lani told her. Just a few acres to start with. Land is cheap and there's plenty of rain. We'll grow everything organic, waste nothing. Turn every square foot into a perpetual garden.

On a bright, breezy day Lani and June followed a pig trail over a 1950s lava flow into the Puna rainforest and found their homestead. Wild pink orchids and night-blooming jasmine grew along a rough, red-earth track fringed by tree ferns and coconut palms. Lehua flowers bloomed, red and frilly, on the soft-leaved 'ōhi'a trees, and an i'o, a Hawaiian hawk, flew overhead. Lani declared it a good omen so they bought two acres, carved out a clearing, and built a small cabin and a catchment tank to collect rainwater. A decommissioned shipping container became a storage shed for tools and fertilizer. Their dining room was a blue tarp stretched between palm trees, sheltering a picnic table. They asked a Buddhist friend to marry them and celebrated with a potluck lū'au.

June's parents sent their apologies and best wishes and a check to cover the cost of the cabin's metal roof.

When Lani saw June's disappointment, he told her "You're part of the 'ohana now. A big new family. Now we have people and wisdom from all cultures. Family is fluid, we are all your 'ohana."

"But what about *your* family?" she'd asked him. He told her he and his parents didn't share the same views about purpose and livelihood. When he'd insisted on using the Hawaiian name Lani instead of his given name Lawrence, refused to attend private school on Oahu, and rejected the idea of working for the family's land development corporation, they'd told him to make his own way in the world. Which Lani was happy to do. He hadn't spoken to his father since high school.

June knew there'd been a phone call from his mother a year ago, informing him that his father had survived a minor heart attack. What Lani had done with that information, he wouldn't say.

Everything about homesteading was harder than June expected, and it all took time: Clearing the rough, uneven land; convincing crops to grow; defending everything from insects and diseases and pigs; getting produce to the local markets before it spoiled. Under a thin skin of red-black dirt, the land in Puna was mostly crumbled crusts and hard ledges of old lava. It was high in iron and it drained well, but it wasn't soil. To create soil, they had to find cheap sources of compost.

Not long after their wedding, Lani told June they need lots of good shit. The real stuff, horse shit.

He had a friend who knew a rancher who kept horses sometimes at Pana'ewa, a public stable next to the county rodeo arena. Every Monday for nearly two decades, Lani and June drove their pickup to Pana'ewa and scooped horse shit direct from the source. That, plus manure from their chickens and every compostable item from daily living, turned the brittle lava into rich, tillable soil. Slowly by slowly, the clearing became a farm.

Gradually, the land also transformed June and she became like Lani: a kamāʻāina, someone "long time on the land." Lani set up tanks to raise catfish and June learned beekeeping. They sold or bartered eggs, coffee, honey, and fruit at the farm markets. June created their Facebook page and Lani blogged about sustainable farming. They named their farm Lani June, the perfect name because "lani" means heaven.

The land structured their first day together, then the next and the next. The days became seasons, the seasons became years. In eighteen years, they were able to create everything except children.

In the beginning they told each other *No rush, the keiki can come by-n-by.* Just in case, June chose names—Leilani, Keahi, Napua—but she never told Lani.

By-n-by never arrived. June's thoughts of children came only occasionally now, late at night when Lani's snoring or the shrill songs of the coqui frogs kept her awake.

There were no babies and now there is no farm. The catfish and honeybees are dead and all their crops— bananas, papayas, rambutan, lilikoi, citrus, sweet corn, coffee, tomatoes, beans, strawberries, edamame, hot peppers—are shriveling in the fumes. Their few remaining hens produce no eggs. When today's sun rises in a few hours, the light will filter through a gray, foul-tasting air. The island belongs to Pele, the powerful and vindictive goddess of volcanoes. Pele gives and Pele takes away.

The current eruption had begun two weeks earlier, after months of seismic warnings. A mushroom cloud of molten rock, ash, and toxic gases erupted from the lava lake in Halema'uma'u, the hundred-thousand-year-old crater at Kilauea's summit.

On the same day, long cracks appeared in the earth. Not in the National Park or a remote rainforest, but right in the center of Leilani Estates, a residential neighborhood twenty miles downslope from the summit, only three miles from Lani and June's farm.

Evacuate now! came the order from HEMA, the Hawaii Emergency Management Agency. *Follow the coastal roads.*

But first to go, HEMA added, must be the people at greatest risk. Others should wait, stay off the roads and shelter in place.

"We're fine," Lani told June. "We can stay."

The next day, as Lani and June worked feverishly to harvest vegetables withering in the foul air, the volcano shook the island with a massive earthquake. Huge fissures split the ground, spewing explosive steam and massive rivers of lava. Their planned escape route, Highway One-thirty, was blocked.

The magma living beneath the island had found the East Rift Zone, a vulnerable seam that runs for four miles beneath farms and neighborhoods. Lava followed the rifts upward, burning and burying houses, ranches, seaside vacation homes, black-sand beaches, and fragile coral reefs.

On the fourth day, June and Lani pulled on their newly issued goggles and breathing masks and walked past homes with well-tended front yards and children's playsets, to where a river of lava was flowing.

A county firefighter stopped them at a line of orange cones and showed them where to stand—only here, no more close, keep your masks on—to watch the lava as it sprayed and fountained from a five-hundred-foot-long fissure in the earth's crust. As they stood there, the molten rock swallowed an empty dog kennel and mounded briefly against the back wall of a two-car garage. The garage and the attached house—newly re-painted, pale gray with pretty lavender trim—burst into flames. Within minutes the buildings were gone, torched by fire and smothered in a twenty-foot pile of cooling rock.

June stumbled to the side of the road, pulled off her mask, and vomited onto someone's lawn.

"Pele must be jealous," the firefighter shrugged under his gear. "She want that house, she take it." He said he'd been there for sixteen hours, moving the barriers to higher and higher ground as the lava spread. "I lost two pair boots. Soles melted right off." He attempted a feeble joke. "I guess Pele needs boots, too."

"That's Melanie Kitasura's house!" June yelled. "She has three kids, where can she go?"

Lani tried to put an arm around her shoulders but she shrugged him off.

"That man, how can he be so callous?" She swiped wet grit from her eyes as they walked home.

"The lava just comes. No one can stop it," Lani said. "His job is to warn us, get us out. Make sure people stay safe."

"But we *aren't* safe."

Civil Defense has distributed a new topographical map with squiggly blue lines showing the "path of steepest descent," where lava is likely to flow when Kilauea erupts. She and Lani live on top of one of those blue lines.

Did that map exist eighteen years ago? Would she have paid attention then?

Before Kilauea blew up, thirty-five hundred people lived above the East Rift Zone on those squiggly blue lines. Nearly all have fled, scrambling to save whatever they could carry away. Farmers rounded up whatever livestock they could find. Some refugees moved in with relatives; others found high-priced rentals in Hilo or Waimea. Most, however, are sheltering in the overcrowded Red Cross centers, or in the tent city that has bloomed in Pāhoa, the nearest town.

If Lani and June had left with the others, they'd be safe now. Maybe they'd be living in Hilo or Kona, maybe working at real jobs.

But Lani had convinced her to stay during the early days and now it's too late. Lava covers all the roads to the northeast. The northwest road, Highway One-thirty, was barricaded by Army engineers after deep cracks split the asphalt and began spewing steam and sulfurous gases.

The few remaining holdouts like Lani and June cannot leave now unless they go on foot along the unmapped pig paths that wind deep into Puna Forest Reserve, where the ground shakes and steam hisses from new fissures.

Lani won't admit they should have left when they had the chance.

"We're staying," he repeats. "We're okay here. The National Guard is fixing One-thirty. They're putting down those steel plates, like bridge pieces. Soon as the earthquakes settle down."

June can only shake her head in defeat.

"Besides," he adds, "someone needs to keep an eye on these people's homes. Chase off the pigs and looters. We stay, keep things safe."

Lani has always tried to keep things safe, but June knows no one can do that here. The danger's not only in the lava erupting from the earth beneath their feet. It's also in the toxic ash that falls from the sky, smothering plants and poisoning animals.

Outdoors, Lani and June wear N-95 air masks, wraparound goggles, long-sleeved shirts, jeans, tall socks, and work boots. Inside, they've taped the windows with plastic and hung tarps over the doors. When the air gets bad, they wear masks indoors, too.

There's also the curious stuff called Pele's hair: fine, wispy tangles of pale, amber-colored fibers shot from pressurized pinholes in the earth's crust. A strange form of lava, like abrasive threads of asbestos or fiberglass, beautiful and lethal. Airborne locks of Pele's hair drift over the blistered landscape, traveling on trade winds and steam fumes. They curl and cling, settling softly and coating everything with delicate, dangerous dust bunnies.

Several times a day, June sweeps up the deadly fluffs of Pele's hair that have found their way into the house. Each evening, she pulls on work gloves and uses a stiff-bristled brush to scrub the sharp, glassy threads from the soles of their work boots. Pele's hair reminds her of Lani's hair if the pale lava threads could be twisted into dreadlocks.

It's the small disruptions that gnaw at a person, not just the cataclysmic destruction. County water lines are broken, power lines have been toppled or melted by lava. Cell service comes and goes.

They still have to eat. This morning's breakfast is simple: their last avocado, reheated rice, a slab of Spam. June adds an oatmeal bar and two half-ripe tomatoes. There's no coffee, so she fills two mugs with water from a jug in the fridge.

Their generator-powered satellite dish still works. The morning news informs them that Highway One-thirty remains closed. More equipment and workers have arrived by barge from Oahu to repair the road. Soon, maybe, the road to Pāhoa will open.

Pāhoa, the only real town in lower Puna, is seven miles northwest of their farm. It has gas stations, schools, churches, a laundromat, a 7-Eleven, a bank, a police station, a community center, a post office, and three restaurants. Also now a Red Cross shelter and a Civil Defense command post.

If they can get to Pāhoa, they can buy food, do their laundry, pick up mail, get gas. *And leave,* June thinks. *Leave, and don't come back.*

Maybe, the news announcer says hopefully, just maybe Highway One-thirty will open tomorrow or the next day. There's a lot of maybes in Puna district.

That's the way it is. On Day One they were told, "Go, leave now!" Two days later: "No, stay, the roads are too crowded, it's not safe to travel." The day after that: "Evacuate!" Then, after new lava vents opened: "No, don't evacuate, too dangerous, shelter in place." Then, "Grab everything and go down that road. No, not that one, go this other way instead."

You can spend three hours crawling through toxic fumes and scalding steam on ground that melts the tires off your car, and then be told to turn around and go back.

June slices the avocado. "As soon as One-thirty opens, we've got to get out. Permanently. We've got to find someplace to live and work."

"But we *have* a place to live. We can't abandon our farm. There will be looters and squatters. The pigs will destroy whatever's left."

She flings her knife into the sink, the avocado forgotten on the cutting board. "Shit, Lani, the *farm?* The farm is all pau, dead and gone. Whatever survives, no one can eat it. Who will buy gray spinach and rotten tomatoes? The ash contaminates the soil, the sulfur kills everything! It's *gone.*"

"We have to rebuild, start again, soon as we can." He places his rice bowl in the sink. "We'll recover, we always recover. Hurricane Madeleine, two years ago? All that flooding. We came back okay."

"For Chrissake, Lani. That was three days of rain and wind. How can you compare that to this? We have no idea how long before the soil is good again, or how to fix it. All our savings will be gone in a month. We still have truck payments. How do we pay medical bills? No bank will lend us money. How far into debt do we have to fall?"

Lani looks wounded. "We'll be okay, I promise."

June slaps the countertop, hard. "You can't promise anything you can't control!" Then, pleading, "I loved our farm, too, but now it's dead. We can't do this alone. What about your parents?"

"You know that's not gonna happen."

"Then you stay! I'll get a job somewhere. Maybe over in Kona. I can clean houses, do landscaping at a hotel. Then we can keep us going."

He's not listening. "We need to get the land back in shape. Buy seeds and plants, be ready when the lava stops. FEMA will help."

He's digging in, the way he always does, so her voice sharpens again. "And when will the lava stop? Months, years? Maybe never. The soil is poisoned." She pauses. "You're not feeling it, are you? My desperation."

"Desperation? No, don't be like that. We gonna get through. This is our home, our life." He lifts a hand toward her shoulder.

She pulls away. "That's your plan? Tough it out and sleep with your gas mask on? That's not a plan."

She pushes her chair back and folds her arms, closing herself off or holding herself together. Both.

Silence and stalemate.

He shrugs and picks up his shotgun. "Time for patrol." Despite the sulfur fumes, Lani finds he can breathe easier outdoors.

He has appointed himself the watchman of their abandoned community. Each day, he walks whatever farm tracks and forest roads seem safe, carrying a water bottle, a phone, and a gas mask. And the gun, in case something needs to be driven off or killed.

He visits the few remaining neighbors, looking for trespassers and kicking away embers that might start brush fires. Whenever his phone works, he texts photos of stray dogs and cats to help locate their owners.

While he's gone, June scatters corn for their five surviving hens. She keeps them locked inside so they can't dig for bugs in the poisoned soil. There are no eggs to collect.

As she closes the coop, she hears snuffling and grunting in the woods behind their house. The pigs are roaming again, searching for food. Something is drawing them to Adam's house. It's closed up now but perhaps he left a garbage can outside, and the pigs are scavenging for scraps.

Adam is a small, frail man in his eighties, a once-tough cattleman who spent most of his life on a ranch in Ka'u, near South Point. He's been their friend for many years, sharing his farming skills and showing them how to craft leis of flowers and feathers to sell to the tourists.

When June spoke with Adam after the first big quake, he'd resigned himself to moving in with his niece, up the Hāmākua coast. "I do not argue with the goddess of the volcano," Adam told June. "If Madame Pele wants her land back, who am I to tell her no? She is isn't real

the earth-eating goddess."

June understands this better now, the belief in a malevolent goddess who shapes the land and everyone's future. Whatever will be, will be. If no can, no can.

Lani had checked on Adam's house a few days ago. No sign of a break-in, he told her. Windows closed, doors locked. So Adam must be gone up the coast, because when local people are home, their windows and doors are always open. How else would the breezes and the geckos slip in?

June can't remember when she last saw a gecko. And now an open window just lets in the sulfur fumes.

Sometimes, though, when the trade winds swing around to the east, there's a bit of relief. The toxic vog drifts away inland toward Kona and the air clears. Occasionally the roar of the volcano pauses and June remembers how it used to be.

It's that way this afternoon—a little fresher, a little quieter—when Lani calls. She's in the kitchen, wiping ash film off the counters.

"Good news!" He's almost singing. "The road's opening! We can go to Pāhoa tomorrow."

"Oh!" June drops into a chair, giddy with relief. "Oh, yes, that's wonderful! We can get food and gas and do laundry. Listen to that, I'm excited about doing laundry."

Suddenly an afternoon rain shower is pounding on the cabin's metal roof and the air feels fresh and wet. A minute later, the sky clears and the late afternoon sun slants in. June spots a rainbow hanging low in the eastern sky. This is the land of rainbows—nearly every day brings a shower, and every shower has a rainbow—but since the eruption, vog has smothered the rainbows. She smiles as she pulls back the grubby square of plastic that covers the window above their mattress.

As Lani heads for the outside sink to wash, June tunes the receiver to a local music station, then rummages through the kitchen, pulling out small bits of food they've been saving. Tonight, they'll have the last of the rice and Spam. There's a can of beer they can share and a few stale crackers and a small square of chevre the Kea'au goat lady gave them just before the lady and her goats escaped north to Kurtistown.

When Lani comes in, damp and smelling of soap, she greets him with a smile and an open-mouthed kiss. She's clean, too, and her hair smells of shampoo.

When had they last made love? Their passion for each other has been slipping away for years; she can't blame that on the volcano. But maybe she can make it up to him tonight.

Delighted, Lani pulls her in and kisses her back. "A celebration, all this, just for a trip into town?"

"It's like being let out of prison. After so long!"

"It's not so long, just two weeks. We've gone that long before, between trips to town." He seems surprised that so little can make her happy.

"But this is different." Doesn't he understand how trapped she feels? No matter. Tonight will be good and tomorrow will be better.

That night, they recognize each other's strong brown bodies, and they make love by the silver light of a half-grown moon. They fall asleep naked and unmasked, tangled in sheets and each other, while the wild pigs run unhindered through abandoned gardens and dead forests.

****

Early the next morning, Lani loads the pickup with fuel cans and water jugs. On the dashboard, he places extra masks and their Local Resident placard that allows them to drive through the restricted areas. He wants to go early, be there when everything opens.

"But first," June says, "please check on Adam's house. Maybe there's garbage there, something that the pigs are getting into. Maybe you can tidy up and scare them off."

Lani picks up the shotgun and heads through the trees to Adam's house. Set in a grove of areca palms, it's a three-room cabin built island-style on square posts and concrete piers with a broad roof overhanging the front lanai.

The pigs have been here. There's a shredded piece of plastic and several empty soda bottles strewn across the front yard. From the gravel driveway, Lani can also see that the front door has been gouged and splintered by teeth or tusks. Something has been trying to get into the house.

When he climbs the steps, he realizes that the wooden door is already partway open, broken off at the top hinge and canted sideways in its frame. At the bottom, there's a gap big enough for a large animal to crawl through.

Lani holds the shotgun in his right hand, lifts the door with his left, and pushes hard, opening it far enough to step through.

The putrid smell hits him. Not garbage, something much worse. Decay and blood, mixed with excrement. He hears the steady drone of flies.

He claps a hand to his mouth and braces himself, dreading what he will find.

What used to be Adam Tanaka is splayed on the kitchen floor. An old revolver rests beside the body. There's a large brown stain, sticky-looking and busy with flies.

The pigs have been here.

Lani gags and reels backward. He forces the door off its remaining hinge and escapes, dropping the shotgun on the lanai. Breathing in great gulps of sulfur-tainted air, he leans against a post until the blood stops pounding in his head.

That's not Adam, that can't be Adam.

Adam showed us where to pick limpets off the rocks in Kapoho. Adam tried to teach me 'ukulele but I was too clumsy, so I never practiced. Adam is safe, living with his niece in Hāmākua.

But he'd recognized the denim shirt, Adam's favorite. And Adam's wire-rimmed glasses, neatly folded on the kitchen counter.

June talked about feeling desperate. But this is what despair really looks like.

He turns away. He's got to move fast, so what does he need? A hammer, nails, plywood, to seal up Adam's house and keep the pigs out. It's the best he can do. He'll report it when they get to Pāhoa. This isn't an emergency, not now. He picks up his shotgun and heads home.

June is busy stuffing clothes and towels and sheets into a canvas laundry bag so she doesn't see Lani walk behind the chicken coop.

He carries tools and a half-sheet of plywood to Adam's house and nails the door shut. He blinks back hard tears as he fastens plywood, thinking the whole time about Adam. And about June.

***

"You checked on Adam's place?" she asks. Lani turns the pickup onto the highway, and they join a line of other slow-moving vehicles heading into town.

"Damnit," Lani says. "Can't they go faster? Where did all these cars come from?"

June is staring out the side window and has forgotten her question. Clouds of stinking steam and dense smoke float by them. She flinches from the concussion of invisible explosions and hears the crackling of unseen fires.

This isn't real, she thinks. *It's a movie set for a post-apocalypse film where the burnt, broken landscape tells you immediately that there will be no saviors and no survivors.*

Yet here they are, heading into town to do laundry.

Lani leans forward and peers into the smoke, guiding the truck carefully around potholes and steam vents, and over the huge steel plates laid down by the DOT and Army engineers.

She remembers her question. "Is Adam's house okay?"

"Yeah, it's secure. All locked up. There was—some trash, out front."

"That's what the pigs were after. It's good you took care of it."

Then they're out of the sulfur clouds and approaching the next checkpoint, where a state trooper nods at the card on their dashboard and directs them to the high-school soccer field, now a sprawling refugee camp. They park next to the community center's pool, now murky with fallen ash. Four goats and a horse are tied to the chain link fence.

June gets out and stares. Hundreds of people are living here in cars and vans, under tents and tarps. Dogs and babies sprawl on blankets. Electric cables for grills and refrigerators snake over the mud. Everywhere, people are waiting in lines for news, mail, water, food. Waiting to be contacted, processed, fed, interviewed, reunited.

Children cry, dogs bark, goats bleat. People argue and scream and weep. The smells of brimstone and barbecues compete.

June spots a woman sitting on the tailgate of a pickup, grilling breakfast on a hibachi. One hand wields a metal fork, prodding sausages, and the other holds a phone. "Yes," June hears her say, "the graduation was lovely. We couldn't be prouder. Four-point-oh, full scholarship to UCLA. He's trying to decide, history or political science."

June remembers: It's high school graduation time. How perfectly normal.

Lani bumps her shoulder and reminds her to line up for the laundromat. "I'll get gas and chicken feed. You can start the wash, then go to the post office." He pushes the bulging laundry bag into her arms and gives her a gentle shove.

June moves a few steps forward and watches as their pickup disappears around a curve. She drops the laundry bag in the mud, sits on it, and pulls out her phone.

If it's eight o'clock volcano time, it must be two PM Connecticut time.

One mile to the west of the refugee camp, Lani pulls up to a gas pump. As he pumps the gas, Lani thinks now that June is right, they need to leave. He's not sure where they can go, but they will talk about it. Maybe north to Kohala. They can lease some land and start farming again, far from the volcano. He smiles and thinks of their lovemaking the night before.

Seven thousand miles to the east, June's mother answers her phone.

Lani pays for the gas, then pulls out his phone and calls June but it goes to voicemail. He doesn't know what to say so he doesn't leave a message. After a long moment, he calls his father.

As Lani is driving to the feed store, June is flagging down a car heading toward the airport in Hilo. In the car, she calls Lani but the call goes to voicemail. She isn't sure what to say so she doesn't leave a message.

By nine in the morning, Lani has found the abandoned laundry bag in the soccer field and June is in the airport lounge, waiting for her interisland flight to Honolulu. She knows where she's going: Honolulu to San Francisco, San Francisco to Chicago, Chicago to New York. Her father will pick her up at JFK and drive her home, to Bridgeport. She might make it in time for dinner, tomorrow evening.

Waiting on a hard plastic chair for her flight to board, she folds an ankle over one knee and uses a ragged fingernail to dig a clump of Pele's hair from the tread of her boot.

In Honolulu, she'll have time to buy new shoes, a toothbrush, underwear. In Honolulu, she'll try calling Lani again, too. Maybe.

Fathering

She leaves the ice cream shop early and drives to the school at the designated time, with her white shirt and black jeans still reeking of sugar and cream. Picking up their son isn't usually her job, but right now all the jobs are hers.

She speeds, just a little, on the empty straightaway past the hillside pasture where red cows graze behind a tumbled-down stone wall. The wall is topped with rusted barbed wire strung haphazardly from crooked posts.

Calves, she thinks. He will want to see the babies.

She won't arrive early but she won't be late, either. She must be on time.

Her boy sits alone on a gray wooden bench outside the brick-faced primary wing, his battered red backpack next to him. For just a moment, she watches him as he swings his feet and eyes the other second-graders, swirling in bright clusters behind the schoolyard's chain link fence.

She angles the car into a space and steps out to open the curbside rear door. He runs to her, bumping his pack against her hip as he slings it into the back seat. He scrambles in and sits in the middle. When she climbs behind the wheel, their eyes connect in the rear-view mirror. She smiles.

"Seatbelt, please."

He buckles up, fidgets and sniffs. "Maple walnut?"

"Butter pecan. I had to open a new tub today."

"I knew it was something nutty. I like chocolate better. Where's Dad? How come he didn't pick me up?"

"He's still in Montreal, remember? The sales conference is over but he still has a few more things to do. He said he'll be home in four days. Sunday, if he can get the flight he wants."

"Oh yeah, I forgot." He was silent for a moment. Then, "Miz McKeon showed me where that is, Montreal. On the Canada map. She said people speak French there."

"I think most people up there speak French. You've learned some French."

"I can count in French! Miz McKeon taught us. *Un duh twa cat sank seez set.*" He says it fast, slurring the words together. "But I don't think Dad speaks French."

She glances in the rear-view mirror. His forehead is scrunched up, worried-looking. "When you see him, you can ask him. He'll be impressed, you learning French."

"Oh look, there's another new calf! That's five. Can we stop?"

She pulls off the pavement onto grass and gravel, avoiding the deep ruts near the sagging gate where tractors have churned the mud.

He climbs out and stands beside the front bumper, smiling. Behind the rock wall and the barbed wire, a dozen russet-colored cows stare back, twitching their dirty rope-like tails and slinging their massive heads to fling away the black flies. A day-old newborn and four older calves peer from behind their mothers' bulky bodies.

"Mmmmuhhh," her boy says softly. "Mmmmuhh." He mimics the cows' soft calls, the way his mother has taught him. The momma cows lower their heads and stare in silence. They shuffle their feet but stand their ground. Then one responds with a soft, guttural murmur, and the boy flashes his mother a grin.

She's proud because he remembers to move quietly so the cows aren't spooked. She opens her car door wide, so he can hear her.

"Good for you, you remembered how to talk to them. Watch the mud."

He nods and approaches the stone wall in slow, gliding steps.

Her phone vibrates in the cupholder, signaling a text from her husband's work number.

A single word: Hey.

Her heart flies up and opens, as it did when they were new together, half a dozen years ago in another muddy spring like this one. When he was sending fervent messages of wild love, a dozen times a day, with bluebirds and hearts and roses attached to every thought.

Before she can respond, another text arrives. This one will have roses attached, she thinks. There must be roses.

Sorry, can't get home til Wed earliest. No flights. Don't try to call. No cell service this weekend.

No hearts, no roses, no bluebirds.

Another:

BTW Montreal is wonderful now! But I need to spend more time here. A month at least in December or January.

There's a new project, temp but maybe perm. I need to see if I can live here year-round. Talk when I get back.

She exhales sharply. The coward! He's doing this by text? She types.

WTF?? What about us?? Your family?? Don't we get a choice?

She clears it. Types instead,

We miss you! Call me now? Love you.

She pauses, adds a single heart, and sends it.

Her son's voice floats in from near the stone wall. "Mom, the father isn't here. Where's the daddy cow, the bull?"

Her face is hot and angry. But her son doesn't see, he's still watching the cows. She organizes an answer.

"They take the bull away while the babies get born, so the momma cows don't get distracted. Then they can do a good job taking care of the calves. In the fall, the bull comes back to the field to help the cows make next year's babies. It takes nine months for a cow to grow a baby, same as people."

She adds, "The farmers plan it that way. They want to have the calves born in spring when it's warm and there's lots of grass. May and June are good months."

"Like me, I was born in June. Next month I'll be eight!"

"Yes. The bull will come back in August, probably."

She glances at her phone. Nothing. She calls his number but it goes to voicemail.

"I'll be in third grade then," her son says. He points. "See the littlest calf? His momma keeps him away from the others, so he won't get stepped on." The newborn nurses, bracing itself on spraddled stick legs and shoving its muzzle hard against the cow's pale brown udder.

"Yes," she says. "She's doing a good job of mothering."

"The bull should be here too," he states firmly. "So he can do a good job of fathering."

She half-smiles. "That's not what the word—"

"Dad's coming home Sunday, right? You said."

She checks her phone again. No more texts, no new calls. She has nothing but the small news she doesn't want to give him. She has to say something.

"Your dad texted just a few minutes ago. He can't get a flight Sunday. Tuesday or Wednesday, he thinks."

She tightens her mouth against thoughts she shouldn't be having. *Tuesday or Wednesday? Unless he volunteers to stay even longer. Because he's having such a lovely time or he met someone at the conference or in a bar, and he's conveniently forgotten us. Again.*

"He also says he might have to go back in the winter. To Montreal, for a month or maybe longer." She says this aloud and immediately regrets it.

Her son twists toward her, the cows forgotten. His eyes are wide. "A whole month? Are we going with him? What about Christmas?"

"We can't go, honey. You'll have school. And it will cost too much for us to stay there. I'd have to quit my job."

And maybe he won't want us there.

She feels the self-pity kick in, followed by the shame of giving in to it. Because you can't do that when you're a mother. You have to protect your kid, not enlist him in your cause.

"Call him! Did you call him?" His face goes wet with quick hot tears. "What if he doesn't come back? We have to go! I'll learn more French. *Un duh twa cat sank seez set!*" he shouts. "I got to seven, what's eight? What's next?"

Before she can respond, he crouches and grabs a handful of mud from underfoot. He spins, hurling it with all his small boy's strength over the rock wall and into the herd of cows. The clod smacks against a heifer's neck.

Panicked, the cows wheel and scatter, shouldering and stumbling into each other. The tiniest calf staggers and nearly falls. The mother cow wheels and braces herself, head down, preparing to charge but not knowing which way to go.

"Be careful. Get in trouble and you die." That's what her best friend Stefanie had told her. Liz assumed she didn't mean it literally.

Nine-year-old Liz Walters knew the old playscape was off-limits and had been for years. She hadn't planned to climb the ladder. This was just going to be a reconnaissance mission.

By mid-afternoon on a Friday in late August, she'd crossed Johnson's cow pasture and was standing behind the closed-up village school, contemplating the sad condition of its abandoned playground.

All around her, the tail-end of a western Massachusetts summer was on display. Vivid, red-fruited sumac bushes leaned over stone walls and, above, the deep jade-green leaves of the sugar maples brandished hints of flame and gold. The folded hills and shaded, hidden ravines of the Berkshires stretched on all sides of the valley.

Liz nibbled on a much-chewed thumbnail and ignored the photo-ready landscape. Her mission was to survey the playscape and report back.

"I can't go to the playground with you tomorrow," her best friend Stefanie told her the night before. "I've got that swim meet at the lake. I'm sorry, I forgot about that." Then she'd added, kindly, "If you want to check it out by yourself, go ahead. I won't mind. Maybe take some pictures? Tell me what you find and we'll go back, together, later on. But don't tell anyone, don't get in trouble."

After watching ninja contests on TV, Stefanie had convinced Liz that they should fix up the old playground so they could create their own warrior-ninja games. They'd hold competitions and sell tickets. Of course Stefanie and Liz would win every time, because they were going to practice every day. They would also design the courses and make the rules. That, Stefanie had declared, would be super awesome.

Stefanie had turned ten a week earlier. She was four months older than Liz, three inches taller, and supremely confident. If Stefanie was suggesting a solitary scouting mission, then of course Liz would go.

After an early breakfast, Liz had pulled on her usual summer clothes—a well-worn t-shirt with denim shorts and a pair of sneakers. Not sneakers, she reminded herself. What Stefanie called them: running shoes. She filled the water trough and carried hay to Belle, her Jersey heifer. She topped off the hens' feed bin with cracked corn, collected a half-dozen eggs, helped her mom fold laundry, and ate lunch. If her dad had been home she'd have helped him organize tools and supplies and clean out his electrician's van, but he was away wiring new homes in West Stockbridge.

Her cousin Joey was coming by later to fix a leak in the roof of the chicken coop, and he'd probably stay for dinner, but that was hours away.

"Go on, get out of my hair," her mother said as she set a frozen chicken on the counter to thaw. "No TV or videos. It's a nice afternoon, go outside and play."

Liz wasn't thinking about television or videos. "Okay if I walk to the school?"

"All right. You have your phone? Get back by four, don't be late. If you're going through the pasture, don't step in the cowpatties. Take Pepper if he wants to go."

Liz wanted to give her mother an eye-roll for the cowpatties remark but didn't dare. Yes, she had her old flip-phone and no, she wouldn't step in cowshit. She wasn't a baby. And jeez, couldn't her mother say *cowshit*, just once? Or *cow manure*, at least.

Pepper, their very old cattle dog, didn't want to go anywhere. He was content to stay in the shade beside the chicken coop, dozing and pretending to be on guard duty in case a coyote threatened the hens.

It was only a ten-minute walk if she cut through Johnson's pasture. For kindergarten, first, and second grade, Liz's mom had driven her the half-mile to the six-room village school. They'd walked along the road when the weather was fine. After Stefanie had moved in nearby, a year ago at the start of third grade, the two girls had walked to school together, going cross-lots through Johnson's pasture, as the older kids did. Liz knew the trails through the pasture and woods as well as anyone in the neighborhood.

Stepping out of the woods behind the school, she paused next to an old equipment shed and briefly considered the shed's contents: a piece of broken snow fence, a rusted shovel, and some unidentifiable small-engine parts. Nothing here that would be even remotely useful for ninja games. Mouse droppings littered the shed's hard clay floor and tangles of dusty spiderwebs clung to the rafters. Liz brushed away a lace of cobwebs that drifted against her cheek.

The Dublin school, a two-story white structure with shuttered windows and peeling paint, stood a few hundred yards away, next to the paved two-lane road. The building was no longer of any interest to her. She'd been a student there for four years, but she wouldn't be going back.

The old family farms were failing, her dad said, so people were selling out and moving away. Dublin wasn't even a village, more of a crossroads, a hiccup between two roads that ran north from West Stockbridge to Pittsfield. The few remaining students had been transferred to the larger consolidated school in nearby Richmond. In one week, Liz was starting fourth grade at the new school, where most of the girls would still ignore her and the boys would still call her Lizzy Lizard. At least she'd be in the same class as Stefanie.

Stefanie Jacobson's family had bought the big old farmhouse just up the road. They'd come from Boston, and Stefanie's parents had jobs that required suits and ties. The family's goal, as Stefanie had explained, was to escape the big city and create a "country home that Martha Stewart would be proud of." Liz had only a vague idea of who Martha Stewart was, but she was very impressed with the entire Jacobson family, who were able to own a beautiful farm without being dirt-poor farmers.

Liz was immensely grateful for Stefanie, who was everything that Liz wished she could be: tall and blond, with cute freckles and an easy laugh. Stefanie swam and played soccer. Took ballet, violin, and horse-riding lessons. Around Stefanie, Liz felt small and awkward, all elbows and angles, but Stefanie never seemed to notice. She bounced happily from venture to venture, scheme to scheme, cheerfully towing the admiring Liz in her wake.

Liz was still trying to understand Stefanie's view of adults. In Liz's world, adults were the arbitrary rule-makers who required unquestioned obedience from children. She'd learned early that following rules—keep quiet, do what you're told, don't make a fuss, mind your manners—was the best way to live with the big people. Stefanie never seemed to worry, as Liz often did, about how to move from *child* to *adult*. That gulf seemed so wide.

Stefanie appeared certain that adults were just older versions of herself. Since Stefanie seemed to have found a clearly marked path to adulthood, Liz tried to learn as much as she could from her friend. Stefanie was always asking questions: *What if?* and *Why not?*

The old playscape behind the school had been closed off, Stefanie said, to protect the little kids. Almost fourth graders, pre-teens about to become *young women*, she and Liz were obviously not little kids anymore. Since the school was now closed, if the playground could serve a new purpose for the community, then that would be a good thing, right?

If Stefanie was here today, they'd have already slipped through the hole in the chainlink fence and explored the abandoned playscape.

Liz patted her back pocket, the one with the button flap, to be sure her old flip phone was secure. Then she pushed through a thick stand of goldenrod and foxtails to the sagging chainlink fence that surrounded the playscape. Under an oak tree, she found the spot where someone had cut a hole. She crouched, slipped through, and jogged across a small clearing to the abandoned playscape.

She'd never played here—never been allowed to swing, slide, or scramble up the climbing frame. The playscape had fallen into disrepair years earlier, so adults had fenced it off, padlocked the gate, and declared it unsafe.

The removable parts were long gone: swings, a slide, the trapeze bar, the ropes and rubbery footholds on the climbing wall. What remained was whatever was anchored by frozen bolts or set in concrete: a pair of rusty parallel bars, the vertical planks of the climbing wall, and the tall square posts that still supported a metal cross-bar for the missing swings. At one end of the swings frame, a high platform of warped planks was still attached to four uprights. A wooden ladder, bolted to the side of the frame, gave access to the platform.

She paused at the ladder, caught her lower lip between her teeth, and worked her teeth gently into the soft pad of flesh. Unless she bit too hard, drawing blood or ripping off a cuticle, the chewing helped her concentrate. Now it helped her decide.

She'd planned only to look around, snap a few photos, and report back to Stefanie. But here in front of her was what appeared to be a perfectly good ladder, just asking to be climbed.

She took hold of its upright posts, stepped on the lowest rung, and bounced. It wiggled but felt solid. She took a deep breath and went up quickly before she could change her mind. Eight steps, nearly as high as the ceiling inside her house.

At the top, the platform's planks were weathered and creaky, but still in place. Holding one of the square corner posts, she stood and admired the view. From here, she could see the entire schoolyard and beyond: the rough gravel parking lot, a faded hopscotch pattern painted on cracked asphalt, a rusted pole holding half of a basketball backboard with its netless rim hanging lopsided.

Farther away, above the hazy green hills of Lenox Mountain, below puffy white clouds in a deep blue summer sky, three hawks rode an updraft.

Liz let go of the post and stretched both arms to the sky, turning in a slow circle on the platform. Here she was, the great explorer on a fire tower! A lone traveler in space, the queen of the realm, the warrior princess calling her dragons!

She dropped her gaze, scanned the playground again, and grinned. Stefanie would be pleased because this would be *perfect* for their ninja project. They'd need thick ropes for climbing, new swings, rings, and a trapeze. They'd mark out a racetrack with chalk on the asphalt and use Stefanie's new stopwatch to time everything. After several weeks of hard training, in secret, they'd be ready to tackle the *real* ninja games. They'd be the youngest girl contestants in history and it would be *awesome*.

The only problem was how to keep it all hidden, so no one could steal their training secrets. The playscape was in full view of the school and the road in front. Liz saw now that she hadn't needed to crawl through the hole in the chainlink by the woods—there was a gap in the fence between the school's side yard and the playground, where a padlocked gate had hung a few months earlier.

Liz looked again at the structure she stood on. There was one ninja exercise that they could practice right away, using the horizontal metal bar that had held the chains for three swings. On this end, the round bar was fastened to the platform she was standing on. At the far end, about twelve feet away, it was attached to the top of the timber frame that had once held a slide.

She'd watched the TV ninjas move along a similar bar. They hung by their hands, then swayed sideways and shifted their grip, hand over hand, to travel the bar's length. She and Stefanie had practiced the same moves on a narrow branch in an old apple tree, just before the branch had split and dropped them both to the ground. This looked much sturdier than that tree branch. If she lost her grip, she'd simply drop four or five feet to the sand underneath, remembering to bend her knees as she landed. She would stick the landing, like a gold-medal gymnast.

She'd have to avoid one spot on the metal bar, near the beginning, where a rusted bolt stuck up. The chain for a swing, long gone, had been attached there.

She kneeled on the platform and planned each move. Take hold, lean forward, slide onto the bar on your stomach. Swing down, hang from your hands, and sway sideways to build momentum. Move a few inches, first one hand and then the other. Remember to breathe.

Liz gripped the rough bar with both hands, took a deep breath, and swung her body sideways over it. She balanced on the bar for a second, then pushed her head and shoulders up and swung her legs down.

There was a sudden ripping sound, and she felt a fierce pain in her left side. Startled, she cried out and let go. *Drop!* her brain told her. *Drop to the ground!*

Her body spun and slid off the bar, but she dropped only a few inches.

There was another sharp sound of cloth tearing.

One side of her t-shirt was caught on the bolt at the top of the bar. The cloth was rucked up under both armpits and wrapped around her shoulders. She was trapped, hung up in the snagged shirt like a rag doll hung on a peg.

Her first thought was to grab the bar, pull herself back up, and try to free the shirt.

The crossbar was too high, out of reach.

Maybe she could slip out of the shirt. But the fabric had twisted up into a thick bundle, wadded up behind her head and holding her weight. The neck opening was pulled taut, not yet choking her but still snug.

Her cell phone was securely buttoned inside the right rear pocket of her shorts. Also out of reach.

Her scraped ribs burned and her jammed shoulders and arms were beginning to ache. She tried to fight the tears but quickly gave in, crying and hiccupping when she realized she could hang there for hours before anyone found her.

She needed to pee. And that was the worst, the most shameful thing of all, because at almost ten years of age, she absolutely did not want to wet herself. She would hold it, she must hold it. And someone *must* come to her rescue.

She was facing the woods and couldn't see the road. It wasn't a very busy road, but someone driving by might see her if they looked toward the schoolyard. If they were driving with the windows down, maybe they'd hear her.

She snuffled a little. Told herself to stop being a crybaby, and began yelling.

"Help!" Louder. "Help! Help me!"

She paused to breathe and listen. Silence.

A warm stream of urine dribbled down inside her shorts, over her ankles, and into her sneakers.

Liz panicked, throwing herself into wild contortions as she thrashed against the tight cloth that bound her. She screamed a furious roar that ripped from her throat and shook her trapped body.

Finally, exhausted and sobbing, she went limp.

A car door slammed. She heard the sound of footsteps on gravel.

"Hey, Lizzy, is that you? Jeez, what happened? Here, I'm gonna get you down."

She knew his voice. She smelled tobacco, diesel fuel, and sawdust.

Then he was beside her, a heavy-set young man in dirty jeans and a denim workshirt. He stepped close, grabbed her around her hips, and lifted her so she could fumble her way out of the snagged shirt. He stood her on the ground and knelt beside her, inspecting the long red scrape on the left side of her naked ribcage.

Liz stood with her legs braced and her eyes closed tight. She drew quick, shallow breaths and fought down the tears until she could stop shaking. Shrinking away from the man's hands, she crossed her arms over her chest and hung her head, chewing furiously on her lower lip.

Her savior was her cousin Joey, twenty years old, her dad's brother's oldest son. She didn't have to open her eyes to see the familiar tobacco bulge in his cheek, his dirty-dark beard-stubble. She knew he wore a sweat-stained black trucker hat, pulled low over small dark eyes, because that's what he always wore.

Joey had rescued her, Joey was family. She should be grateful. She should say, *Thank you for rescuing me.*

But her shame was too sharp.

"Whatcha doing up there, Lizzy? You working on your circus act or something? That was dumb." He caught a whiff of urine, saw the damp shorts, and sniggered.

"Pissed yourself, didn't you? Here, let's see." He reached to tug at the waistband of her cutoffs and she jerked away, red-faced. "Hey, I'm just trying to help. I used to change your diapers, Lizzy baby. Looks like you need changing again." He smirked. "Don't matter. Let's get you home."

Joey grabbed at her ripped shirt, flipped it up and off the crossbar. He held it out, then grinned and waved it over her head just out of her reach until he saw that she was about to cry again. She snatched it from him, yanked it over her head, and crossed her arms again, wrapping herself in the torn fabric.

She thought briefly of running home, sprinting away from him into the woods. But her body ached and her wet underpants chafed. She walked slowly to his beat-up black pickup.

Joey made a big show of placing an oily rag on the truck's bench seat.

"Stay off my upholstery. Keep your wet ass on that," he ordered as he climbed behind the steering wheel. "Does your momma know you're out here? You ain't supposed to be playing on that thing, are you?"

Liz stared at the floor of the truck and shook her head. Joey drove the truck out of the abandoned schoolyard and onto the blacktop.

"Well now. You don't wanna get in trouble with mommy and daddy, do you? I'll say you just got snagged on a bobwire fence out in Johnson's pasture. And maybe fell down on a rock. That's our little secret. Ain't telling nobody, right?" He smirked and patted her bare knee. Liz looked out the window and swiped roughly at her face. Tasting blood from her chewed lip, she sucked on it gently.

I should be glad, she thought.

They'd ground me for a week if they knew I'd been on the playscape. And I don't have to lie to them — Joey is telling the lie, not me.

Is it my lie, if he says it?

***

"Elizabeth," her mother said, right after the fried chicken and before the apple cobbler, "I don't think you thanked Joey properly for helping you off that bobwire and bringing you home today. You are so very lucky that he got off work early and drove by, right when he did. That was truly a miracle, wasn't it? I think maybe the good Lord had a hand in that. So can I hear you say that clearly, please? Say it. 'Thank you Jesus and thank you Joey.'"

She narrowed her gaze and held her daughter eyes. "And please would you stop chewing on the inside of your cheek like that. It makes you look very unattractive, with your face all sideways and your lip swollen up. Have you asked Jesus to help you with that, too, like I said to?"

Marianna Walters made a special point of invoking Jesus's name whenever possible. She thanked Him several times a day for any positive event in her life, large or small. Sometimes it was a true miracle, like when a big oak tree fell in a storm but didn't hit the house. Sometimes it was a smaller blessing, like the invention of hairspray or non-stick baking pans.

Liz was pretty sure Jesus had nothing to do with what had happened today. When they'd walked in, Joey had told her mother that Liz had gotten her shirt stuck on the fence, then fallen against a rock trying to get unstuck. Liz had showered, sprayed the scrape on her ribs with stinging antiseptic, thrown the mangled shirt into the trash, and received a thorough scolding from her mother.

Her father merely scowled from his seat at the head of the table. "That was careless. You know better than to get tangled up on bobwire. You can get tetanus from that."

"Thank you, Joey," Liz whispered. She kept her eyes on her plate.

"Elizabeth, please *look* at the person you're talking to!" Marianna insisted. "I swear, it's not polite to look away like that. People think you're rude. And don't forget Jesus, say thank you to Jesus too!"

"Awwww." Joey's chair creaked as he shifted his bulk. "Little Lizzy's just real shy, ain't she? What's that my daddy says, still waters going deep, right? You got deep water inside you, Lizzy baby?" He reached a beefy hand across the table to Liz's dinner plate and helped himself to the chicken leg that she'd ignored. He grinned and bit into the dark meat with stained teeth. "Sure is good, Aunt Marianna. You always do the best fried chicken."

They all seemed to be waiting for Liz to say something more.

But her mind was elsewhere, trying to process the ease with which Joey had lied to her parents. He was twenty years old, an adult. He should be siding with the other adults, not telling fibs to cover for her.

She'd never thought of Joey as a *boy*, not in the same way that she thought of other boys she knew—classmates, the brothers of friends, the kids in 4H and Future Farmers. Mostly she knew her cousin as something that was always just *there*. He'd worked every summer in the hayfields, before the land by the river was sold off. He helped her father sometimes with electrical work. He fixed fences, painted the shed, mended the roof, cleaned the gutters, and often hung around for lunch or dinner because Aunt Marianna's fried chicken was the best he'd ever had, every time.

Joey's got it tough, her parents often reminded her. His mother died when he was five. His father was in the army, got diagnosed with PTSD, wrestled with addiction. Joey still lived in his father's single-wide trailer off old Route 7 by the boarded-up wire mill. But his father was seldom home. He was in rehab, or doing a job somewhere. Maybe finishing a stint in jail. The adults were vague about that.

Through several years of middle school, Joey had worked summers and weekends on various farms, paying for his room and board with field labor. He'd almost made it to ninth grade. Turned sixteen, dropped out, and got a job stacking two-by-fours at Turner's lumberyard.

"He still needs a family to be part of," her father often reminded Liz. "That's us."

Most of Liz's early memories of Joey had to do with games. Not sports, but clumsy pranks designed to tease little kids. What Joey called "magic tricks," which often involved money but not much magic.

When she was four and he was fifteen, Joey offered her a quarter and said if she was a good girl, she could have it. But if she hadn't been good, he said, then everyone would know because the man on the quarter, Mr. Washington, would cry. Joey held up the quarter and asked, "Have you been a *real good* girl, Lizzy?" She knew she had been good, she was always quiet and obedient, so of course she'd earned the quarter.

Suddenly tears dripped from Mr. Washington's face, and Joey was telling her she must have been bad, but she had no idea why. Much later, she learned that Joey had soaked a small wad of paper in water and held it with his thumb behind the coin, squeezing out the "tears" for his humiliating little game.

When she was five and he was sixteen, he told her to look in his pockets for money. Whatever she found, she could have, because she was his favorite girl cousin. Which was dumb, because she was his *only* cousin. He tucked quarters under the rim of his trucker's cap, then challenged her to knock it off and send the coins cascading to the floor. He stashed half-dollars in his shirt pockets, so she'd have to crawl over his chest. Once, she found a shiny golden dollar, deep in the front pocket of his jeans.

Liz tried not to think about Joey but when she did, she thought mostly of lumps and bulges. A wad of chewing tobacco in his cheek, red acne bumps on his stubbly chin, and a ridge of fat at the back of his neck. A lump on his forearm, where a broken bone had healed poorly after a tractor accident. A thick pad of beer belly hanging over his belt. Sometimes, during those "magic tricks," she'd been vaguely aware of another bulge, lower down in his lap.

Joey had a fuzzy photo on his cellphone of someone he claimed was his girlfriend, but no one had met her. He sometimes said he was waiting for Lizzy to grow up so she could be his girlfriend. Liz's dad always shook his head at that, and her mom frowned, but they usually laughed, too. Joey's just teasing, they said. But who, Liz wondered, would *want* to be Joey's girlfriend? No one she knew.

Liz poked at a pea with her fork, then slid her gray eyes away and fixed her gaze on a spot above the sink, just behind Joey's left shoulder. "Thank you for helping me, Joey," she said softly. "And Jesus," with a side glance at her mother.

Marianna pushed a glossy red curl off her forehead and frowned. She couldn't put a finger on her daughter's tone. It wasn't insolent or defiant. Secretive, maybe. Elizabeth had always been a hard one to figure out. Obedient, but always too serious and far away in her mind, with her sharp little nose stuck in a book. And that nervous tic, chewing on a fingernail or her lip. Still waters, indeed. Like the girl was hiding a darkness in her, even when she seemed good as gold.

Intent on eating, Carl Walters ignored whatever was going on between his wife and his daughter. It had been a long, hard week. He'd agreed to take a job on a construction site more than an hour away, where he had to work ten-hour shifts with crews who didn't speak much English. But the money was pretty good, so Marianna wouldn't have to get a job at Mario's Diner or one of the fast-food joints out by the Mass Pike, like they'd talked about.

Not that Marianna would want to. She was already too busy with projects she'd been assigned by the new preacher at Spoken Word Evangelical. When Carl questioned the money she spent buying flowers for Sunday services and bibles for the homeless, not to mention their regular tithing, Marianna had said he should be grateful for all her work. She was piling up enough credits to get all three of them into heaven, guaranteed.

She always had his dinner on the table and his lunchbox packed when he needed it. Sometimes he wished she'd given him a son, to carry on the family name and take on his electrician business. But he was glad they hadn't had any more children. With insurance and clothes and food, just the one was expensive enough. Though tonight, his one kid didn't seem to be eating much.

He finished his second helping of gravy-soaked mashed potatoes, planted his tanned, muscular forearms on the table, and pointed his fork at his nephew.

"So, Joey. That heifer we've got out there. She's about eighteen months, ready to get bred. Bert Johnson's got a good Guernsey bull. If we can get her bred now, she'll freshen next May. Good time for a calf."

"You need me to help get that cow to Johnson's?" Joey glanced at Liz. "That's Lizzy's 4H project, right? She's tame enough, she'll be easy to handle. We don't need a truck, Uncle Carl. It's just over the hill. We can walk her over." He smiled. "I bet Lizzy can lead her, no trouble."

Liz turned to her dad, quietly imploring. "My heifer's name is Belle. Her name is *Belle*. And she's too young to be a momma cow, isn't she?"

Marianna broke in. "I don't think we need to be discussing the breeding of cows at the dinner table. Really, Carl? Can't this wait until later, after dessert at least?"

"But Belle's too young, isn't she?" Liz kept her eyes on her father.

Joey smirked. "Ha! That heifer's just the right age. They cost money to feed, they've gotta start producing. Get 'em bred young, they learn what their job is."

"Joey's right," Carl said. "Belle is old enough. She's eighteen months, she's coming into heat regular. I've been tracking her cycle. She's ready. I called Bert and he said we can bring her over tomorrow afternoon. We'll leave her there two-three days, then walk her back."

So it was already arranged. Liz knew better than to protest. She pushed her chair back from the table and stood, holding her plate with the remains of her uneaten dinner. To her mother she mouthed, "May I be excused," and turned to the sink.

"Lizzy, wait. We—your mother and I, we were talking," her father said clumsily.

Liz's antenna went up. Conversations outside of electrical work and farming came hard to her father. He believed that explaining things was mostly his wife's job.

But since he'd raised the topic, he needed to finish it. His neck grew red above the collar of his gray electrician's work shirt.

"See, we think you're old enough to be there when Belle and the bull get together. She's your heifer, after all, your 4H project. And this is an important part of farming. The breeding, it's all part of nature. You can see how it happens, and then maybe you can watch when the calf is born in the spring. It takes nine months, you know that."

Joey grinned. Ignoring him, Liz looked to her mom but Marianna only frowned, nodded curtly, and busied herself moving apple cobbler onto dessert plates.

"Get the ice cream, please, Liz," her mother directed. "I think the scoop's in the dish drainer." Then, quickly, "Before you ask, I know you and Stefanie do almost everything together, but she doesn't need to be part of this. Going to Bert Johnson's tomorrow, I mean, with the cow. She's not from a farm family, she wouldn't understand. I don't think her parents would let her go anyway. This is family business. Farm business."

Farm business? Liz knew her father wished he was still a farmer, but all that remained of the Walters' family farm was five acres, a shabby house, two sheds, eight hens, one heifer, and an old cattle dog. Good thing her father got his electrician's license, or they wouldn't have kept even that much.

A *farm* was what Stefanie's family had: nearly a hundred acres of woods and fields and orchards. A sprawling colonial home, a huge red barn, twin silos, and handsome old fieldstone walls. The Jacobsons were restoring the historic house, and Stefanie's dad was going to hire someone from the agriculture college to bring back the orchards and create their vegetable gardens. They were going to have flocks of sheep and goats and learn to make cheese. Best of all, Stefanie was getting a pony. *That* was a farm.

Also, Stefanie already knew way more about sex than Liz did. If Liz was going to have to watch Belle getting bred by the Johnsons' bull, she very much wanted her best friend to be there with her. But apparently, it wasn't to be.

"Will you come too?" Liz asked her mom.

Marianna's face turned a shade brighter than her hair. She handed a dish of cobbler to her husband. "No, honey," she said briskly, "I've just got too much going on, with bible study and choir rehearsal tomorrow, and the church supper on Sunday evening."

Not looking at her daughter, she added, "We can talk about it afterward in private, Elizabeth, if you have questions."

***

"You went over to the playground today? And then what? You took pictures?"

Stefanie's voice was breaking up a little. Liz moved to the far side of her small second-floor bedroom, near the window that was closest to Stefanie's house, hoping that the phone reception would improve. Outside, the setting sun hanging low in a leafy oak tree, near the driveway to the Jacobsons' farm. Stefanie's house was at the end of that long driveway, not quite visible from where Liz stood, but she could see the stone walls and the wrought-iron gates at the entrance, up the hill where the narrow blacktop turned to gravel.

"At the playground. Did you take pictures?" Stefanie repeated.

Liz wouldn't risk humiliation by telling Stefanie about getting stuck on the playscape. And she certainly wasn't going to say anything about wetting her pants.

Instead, she chose a tone of offhand dismissal, hoping to sound halfway bored.

"I didn't take pictures. It's not worth it, it's nothing but junk. All the swings and slides are gone. It's gonna take too much work to make it good."

"Well, that sucks. My dad said he'd build something at our place, but not until next year. And then we'll have to let my horrible brothers use it. They're too little and they're just gonna hurt themselves on it, but Dad says I can't just kick them off, they'll want to play too. Maybe we can find someplace else."

"We can put them to work selling tickets or something." Liz thought it might be nice to have a brother or sister, but Stefanie always insisted that she'd rather be an only child like Liz. Her six-year-old twin brothers, Davey and Gordy, were icky, gross little monsters who ate worms and peed in the flowerbeds to gross her out.

"Really? My brothers? Oh gawd, they'd be useless." Stefanie groaned. She'd nearly perfected the art of audible eye rolls.

A few months earlier, Stefanie had decided they needed a secret sign language. A slight eye-roll meant "Well, *duh!*" and "That's so **obvious.**" A subtle widening of the eyes signaled disbelief. The universal shrug was for "I'm not going all emotional, I couldn't care less." And Stefanie's favorite, a hidden-behind-the-back, barely-there flash of a middle finger for anyone she disliked. Her little brothers often prompted three or four of these secret signals in rapid succession.

Liz had practiced the secret signals, too, but she wasn't brave enough to use them in the presence of adults. Insurrection was new to her.

Now, Liz was hoping Stefanie had forgotten the whole ninja idea. She told her about the plan to take Belle to Bert Johnson's farm the next afternoon.

Stefanie giggled. "So what's the big deal with watching Belle get bred by the Johnsons' bull?"

Liz aimed again for an offhand tone. "It's supposed to be part of my sex education, birds and bees and things. No big deal. That's the point of living on a farm, after all, growing food. Plants and seeds, animals and babies. Reproduction. You don't get milk if your cow doesn't have a calf."

"Yeah, I get that part. What are you going to do with the calf?"

"If it's a girl, we'll sell it, maybe to someone else in 4H who wants to raise a heifer."

"But what if it's a boy, a bull calf?"

"Someone will still want it." Liz knew what happened to the bull calves. They were raised for veal, closed up in small pens and fed milk so the meat would stay tender. Then slaughtered at six months, or sooner.

More questions from Stefanie. "But what if Belle doesn't get pregnant? Sometimes they don't, right?"

Liz also knew what happened to a heifer that didn't produce a calf. Belle, too, would end up at the slaughterhouse.

"I could train her to pull, I guess. Like an ox. Then she'd have a job."

Stefanie snorted. "No way! Who ever heard of a female Jersey ox? You need something big and strong, like those gigantic steers with horns. The red devils that we saw at the fair last month. Jerseys are *little* cows." She giggled again. "So, can I come along, to watch the cows have sex?"

"Not red devils, Red Devons. I thought your pony is supposed to come home tomorrow. That's a lot more fun than doing anything with cows," Liz said. "Besides, my parents said this is family business. You'd probably just laugh or something."

"I wouldn't laugh! Well, maybe I would," Stefanie admitted. "And *yes*, I want to be here when Max arrives. So, tomorrow, it's just you and your parents and old Mr. Johnson? And Belle and the bull, of course. A cow party, with cow sex." She giggled again.

"Me and my dad and Mr. Johnson. And my cousin Joey."

"Yuck, that's awkward. Your cousin is creepy. And so many people, just to watch cow sex!"

Liz sighed. She'd rather talk about the pony, but Stefanie was having too much fun saying "cow sex."

***

Liz was still in pajamas on Saturday morning when her phone sang its Barbie-theme ringtone.

"My pony!" Stefanie squealed. "My pony has arrived! Come meet Max!"

Thirty minutes later, Liz was standing in the Jacobsons' barn, gently stroking the shoulder of the most beautiful pony she'd ever seen. His mane and tail were thick and black, his coat was a sleek russet color, and he had a small white star on his forehead.

She was in love.

The pony turned his head toward her, politely checking her hands for carrots or apples. Liz shivered with delight as his soft muzzle exhaled warm breath. Ever so gently, she wrapped both arms around Max's silken neck, rested her face against his black, spiky mane, and breathed in his delicious scent. Max smelled like a warm puppy but better, like new leather and green grass.

Stefanie nudged her. "Max has the most beautiful eyes in the *world*, don't you agree? His eyes," she persisted. "Look at his beautiful eyes!"

Liz stepped back and nodded, agreeing that his eyes were lovely—large and liquid, dark golden brown and rimmed with thick black lashes.

The gelding shifted his feet in the deep straw, and a haze of dust motes drifted in on hot, damp air, sifting through the high windows of the old fieldstone barn. The dust sparkled, swirling down onto the pony's seal-brown coat. My mother would say it's only pollen, Liz thought, but really it's fairy dust.

Max regarded both girls with good-natured expectancy, waiting for whatever they would bring him—if not an apple, then an enjoyable grooming, or at least a rub and a scratch on his chest or withers.

"He's what we call a black bay," Stefanie said solemnly as if she were a renowned expert instead of the just-turned-ten birthday girl. As if she owned a hundred horses instead of just this one perfect pony. She handed Liz a rubber curry comb and began issuing instructions on how to groom a pony.

"I *know* how to brush a horse," Liz stated. With infinite care, she drew the curry comb in large, firm strokes over

Max's lovely arched neck and broad shoulders. "When can you ride him? Do you ride bareback? How fast can you go?"

"I can't ride him for a couple of days. He needs time to settle in. Mrs. Townsend is coming Monday to give me a riding lesson. She wouldn't let me bring him home until I could at least ride him at the trot without falling off. Which I can do now, of course. But I still have a lot to learn before I can gallop and jump. His full name is Greenfield's Magnificent Max, isn't that a great name? He's a really *valuable* pony, a registered Welsh Cob, so we mustn't mess up his training and confuse him. He's going to teach me everything he knows! Then we can go to horse shows and win lots of blue ribbons! And he's a super good jumper, aren't you, Max?" Stefanie kissed Max's forehead, right in the center of his small white star.

On Monday, you can ride him, thought Liz, *but when can* **I** *ride Max?* She didn't dare ask, not yet.

"Selfies!" Stefanie sang out.

She pulled out her new smartphone, handed it to Liz, and planted a kiss on the pony's warm, velvety nose. Max wiggled his muzzle and snorted softly, almost sneezing, but he tolerated all the silliness remarkably well, Liz thought. Not like the cranky old quarter horse owned by the Fancher boys up the hill, that they sometimes rode to help move their dad's beef cattle through the fields. That horse would try to kick or bite every time you got near. Liz had ridden him once in a big western saddle and several times bareback. She'd never fallen off.

"Can I come back tomorrow to see Max? I'll help clean his stall and brush him again," Liz offered.

"Tomorrow is Sunday. Don't you always have church stuff to do? If you can't come tomorrow, then come on Monday and watch my riding lesson."

"So you're going to feed Max every morning and evening? And clean his stall every day, right?"

"Oh—yes, I guess I'll have to get up early, especially when school starts, won't I?" Liz thought Stefanie might not have given much thought to that part—feeding, scrubbing water buckets, mucking out the stall, brushing Max, combing the tangles out of his tail, picking out his feet. All those things that Liz was aching to do.

Stefanie tucked her phone back in her jeans pocket and skipped down the barn aisle, leaving Liz to latch the stall door. "Come on, I'll show you Max's saddle and bridle! I got a new saddle pad, too. Pink! It matches my riding helmet!"

***

Later that afternoon, Liz slipped the rope halter over Belle's head and tied her to a post beside the shed. She ran a curry comb over the heifer's fawn-colored coat and used a stiff brush to sweep off the dirt and loose hair. Belle stood placidly, blinking her dark Jersey-cow eyes and swinging her long, ropey tail at the flies that gathered on her back and belly.

"You're a big girl now, you've got to look nice for your date," Liz told her. But she felt stupid saying it, and she was worried. Belle was a small cow, even for a Jersey. Johnson's Guernsey bull was at least a foot taller and two hundred pounds heavier than Belle. It just didn't seem right.

She knew most dairy farms used artificial insemination to breed their dairy cows. She'd seen that once at a neighbor's farm, where she watched the local veterinarian walk down a line of cows locked in their milking stanchions. He'd stuck his gloved arm right up to the shoulder into each cow's vagina and used a long, thin tube to squirt in the bull semen. It was gross and messy, but the cows didn't seem to mind, and it did look efficient. That method also sounded safer than having a big bull jump on top of a little cow. But she knew that anything involving a visit from a veterinarian would be expensive.

Her father stepped off the back porch, pulling on a pair of leather work gloves. He handed a broomstick to his daughter, untied the rope, and led the heifer toward the road. Belle walked a few steps, then swung her head up and planted her feet. She mooed, a distressed "mmmuuuhhh" sound from deep in her throat.

"She needs convincing," her father said. "Pop her on the butt with that stick, Liz. Joey's meeting us at Johnson's," he added. "He'll drive us back. But you and me have to get her there first."

Liz tapped Belle on her hindquarters, first lightly and then a little harder, and the cow lurched forward. Together they maneuvered Belle down the gravel driveway, past the mailbox and the Thank You Jesus sign and the mailbox, and onto the asphalt.

At Johnson's farm, her father dragged Belle into a small holding pen near the back of the barn. He pulled off the rope and she began circling nervously, pausing to pee every few minutes. The bull was in the next pen, on the other side of a high-timbered fence built from old telephone poles and railroad ties.

He was massive, almost twice the size of Belle, with thick stubby horns and a blocky, red-and-white body. When he spotted the cow through the planks of the fence, he bellowed, pawing the ground and slamming his shoulders against the timbers. He shoved his muzzle into a gap between the boards and smelled the heifer with a curled-back lip. His thick, pointed tongue flipped out and back into his wet nostrils. Liz stared into Belle's pen from outside the gate. She felt something crawling through the pit of her stomach, threatening sickness.

Liz's father climbed to the top of the fence to sit next to Joey, who was hunched forward with the heels of his work boots hooked over a rail.

"Hey, Uncle Carl." Joey spat tobacco juice, grinned down at Liz, and started to say something she couldn't hear. Her father elbowed him in the ribs, scowled, and shook his head.

Bert Johnson was a small, wiry, balding man in a long-sleeved denim workshirt and ancient, manure-crusted overalls. He stood next to the fence, watching the cow and bull with a deeply wrinkled, expressionless face that said he knew everything about breeding cows and nothing else was worth discussing.

"Well," Bert said after a few minutes, "She looks ready." He yanked hard on a frayed rope that lifted the latch on the steel gate between the pens.

The bull bellowed and surged through the opening. He slammed into Belle's hindquarters and clambered up onto her back. The heifer staggered forward, almost falling. The bull's hind legs churned as he tried to hold his position. His heavy head and neck hung low over Belle's left shoulder. The heifer's knees buckled.

Liz felt like she'd been punched in the gut. Balling her fists, she turned to her father. "He's hurting her! Stop it, make it stop!"

The three men stared into the pen. No one looked at her.

"Ah, don't worry, Lizzy," Bert finally said. "She'd stronger than she looks. That's a sturdy one, she's okay."

The bull had trapped Belle against the fence. He shoved hard, and then it was over. He slid off the cow and strolled toward a bale of hay in the corner of the pen, shaking flies off his face. Belle stood for a moment, dazed and splay-legged. Then she joined the bull, munching hay and switching her tail at the flies.

Joey and Liz's father dropped off the fence. They both shook Bert Johnson's hand and Bert nodded. No one said anything more.

Her stomach roiled and ached, but the rest of her was numb. She wiped her eyes with the back of one hand and climbed slowly into Joey's truck. She sat in the middle of the bench seat, making herself as small as possible to avoid touching either man. The cab stank with the usual farm smells of diesel, manure, and animal sweat. She became aware of another odor, also: a rank stink that made her scalp prickle. That's the bull, she realized. It's the smell of the bull.

Back in her room, Liz sat on her bed for a long time, chewing on her lip and thinking of nothing in particular. When the taste of blood turned sour and her lip felt sore, she walked to the bathroom, peeled off her clothes, and stepped into the shower. She scrubbed her skin nearly raw and stayed under the spray a long time, until her stomach quieted and the ache in her side went numb and all the hot water was gone.

***

In Liz's family, Sunday mornings belonged to church services at Spoken Word Evangelical. Liz didn't have an opinion about churchgoing—it was simply what you did on Sundays. The music was pleasant and the sermons predictable, so she could sit with her own thoughts. From an early age, she'd learned the valuable art of stillness. She knew that as long as she didn't fidget or chew her fingernails or her lip or the inside of her cheek, no one would bother her.

After lunch and chores, her dad left in his van to fix someone's electrical problem and her mother enlisted her help cooking spaghetti sauce for the evening charity supper at the church. There was no time to visit Stefanie and the wonderful pony, but in the late afternoon she managed a quick phone call.

"So how did it go, the breeding?" Stefanie sounded serious and conspiratorial. No more giggling about cow sex.

Liz sat cross-legged on her bed and struggled for words. "It was … scary. It looked painful. And dangerous, like the bull was angry and wanted to kill her. He sort of smashed her up against the fence. And he was a *lot* bigger. And it was over really fast. It was … violent."

"Well, that's just lust, not love," Stefanie pronounced.

"What do you mean, lust?"

"That's what animals do, silly. It's called hormones, what their bodies tell them to do. Lust-sex is for animals, love-sex is for humans. What my mom says is, when people do it right, they are supposed to talk and get to know each other and agree that they're in love. They should want to get married, before they have sex. Though not everyone gets married. But they both have to want the sex, otherwise it's just lust like the animals and then it's just lust, and you've got to say no, stop, I don't want to."

"How would you make a boy stop? If he wasn't listening or didn't want to."

"I'd crow."

Liz thought Stefanie must've misunderstood the question. Or she wasn't hearing correctly. "You'd what?"

"I'd start crowing." She demonstrated, loudly. "Cock-a-doodle-do! Then I'd laugh and point to his doodle-do."

"His penis." Liz and Stefanie had promised each other to always use the correct terms. Sex was a serious topic.

"Well, duh. His penis," Stefanie agreed. "But I'll bet if I crowed and called it a doodle-do, he'd be so *humiliated* he'd just leave me alone."

"I don't think that would work." Liz was thinking, *It sure wouldn't have worked on Jacobson's bull.*

Stefanie went back to delivering important details about the biology. "And if the sex is to make a baby, the girl has to start her periods first. Like, we are *way* too young."

"But Katie Harvey started, right? She's nine."

They were silent for a moment, thinking sober thoughts about Katie Harvey. Wondering what it must be like to have your insides begin to swell and bleed. To be nine years old and have your body tell you that it's ready for sex.

"But," said Stefanie firmly, "I don't ever want to have sex *anyway* because it's just plain gross. The whole part where the boy puts his penis in you, that's just yucky. Like *eeeww*. I mean, really? Who decided that *that's* the best way to make babies?"

Liz knew she should say, *God decided, that's who. So it must be okay, that's the way it's meant to be. At least when you're married.*

But she didn't say it because she'd been thinking lately that she wasn't so sure about God anyway. If there was a god in charge of these things, then he should have designed a nicer way to make babies. More loving, less violent.

Less terrifying.

"Anyway," Stefanie said in her most adult voice, "It's good that Max is a gelding. Geldings make the nicest riding horses, Mrs. Townsend says, because they have those baby-making parts, the testicles, removed. So they aren't interested in sex with the mares. Only a stallion can do that."

She added, "I almost forgot. Ten o'clock tomorrow morning, that's when Mrs. Townsend is coming. Come watch my riding lesson on Max."

Liz heard her mother's step on the stairs. "Time to go, girls. Elizabeth, they're waiting for us at the church."

***

By seven o'clock on Sunday evening, Liz was tired of serving spaghetti to elderly churchgoers. It was the same spaghetti dinner she'd helped serve to the same two dozen old people, every third Sunday of every month, for as long as she could remember. Spaghetti night was always a grim affair. No music, no conversation, just slimy pasta and sauce distributed quickly with lots of "Thank you, Jesus" and "Praise the Lord" murmurings around the church hall.

"Meatballs or plain?" she asked the slow-moving congregants who shuffled through, some with canes or walkers, balancing food trays topped with paper napkins and plastic handbags.

Liz was supposed to add, "Praise Jesus!" with each serving, but it sounded false, piling Jesus on top of the spaghetti. She dutifully scooped a puddle of runny red sauce onto each plate of limp, overboiled noodles that her mother passed to her. She topped the mound with exactly three heavily breaded meatballs, or not, and handed the plate over into shaky, gnarled hands.

Next to her stood the salad server, a skinny seventh-grade boy with glasses and pimples who showed his braces in a smile or a grimace, she wasn't sure which, each time she looked his way. And his mother, the Jello lady, offering two flavors. Green or yellow, with or without whipped topping.

The red sauce made her think of blood. The meatballs and pale, fat noodles reminded her of other things.

She thought she might be sick, right there in the serving line.

Marianna frowned at her daughter and felt her forehead with a vinyl-gloved hand. "Go get a glass of water and sit in the front hall. The doors should be open, maybe there's a breeze." Then she added, more kindly, "I hope you're not getting sick. We're almost done. Another hour or so for cleanup, and then we can go."

Liz felt sweat beading on her forehead. "Can't someone take me home now? I don't feel so good."

"Your daddy's still out, trying to get power back at that grocery in Richmond. I'll call Joey, he can come get you."

Ten minutes later, sitting in the church foyer away from the smell of spaghetti sauce and the overcooked air in the hall, Liz felt better.

Joey was dressed nicely, for once, in clean black jeans and a pale blue nylon shirt with a bowling team logo over the front pocket. He assured Marianna that she could take her time at the church. He'd get Liz home and make sure she was ready for 8:30 bedtime.

Good, Liz thought. She'd have time to read another chapter or two of her *Saddle Pals* book. If her mom didn't get home until nine, she might be able to stay up late and read even longer.

Joey parked behind the house and switched off the ignition.

"Thanks for bringing me home," she remembered to tell him.

"No problem. Anything for my favorite girl." He said it seriously, not smirking the way he usually did. "I'll just hang out in the kitchen, see if your dad's got any cold beer. Do you have the key?"

He waited on the back porch steps while Liz retrieved the spare house key from under a flowerpot. The August evening sun was below the horizon, early twilight, and her mother had left the back porch light on.

Pepper raised his head and thumped his tail under the kitchen table but didn't get up. Liz headed upstairs. She used the bathroom and changed into her shorty PJs, then turned on her bedside lamp and settled under the sheet with her book.

The bedroom door opened. Joey appeared, silhouetted in the bright light from the hallway.

"Hey Liz. I know you're a big girl, you can get yourself to bed. I just thought I'd make sure you're all set. Give you a little hug and a kiss goodnight, okay? Like I used to when you were a little kid." He half-stifled a beer belch. She closed the book on her chest, pulled the sheet higher, and willed him to go away quickly.

"I'm fine, Joey. Good night. You can close the door and leave. Please."

Joey closed the door but he was already inside. He moved to her bed and leaned down, peering at her book. "Oooh, looky. What a surprise, a book about horses. Girls love horses." He tugged the book from her hands and set it on the nightstand. "What's that song? Oh yeah."

He began in a falsetto. "*All the pretty little horses ...*" He stopped and scratched a red bump on his chin. "Hey Lizzy baby, help me out here. I don't 'member the words."

His giggle changed to a snort as he sat heavily on the edge of her narrow bed.

She scrambled away, acutely aware of his bulk that took up so much space on her small bed. The far side of the bed was right against the wall and she was trapped. Wherever she moved, he could reach her.

"Come on, give me a kiss, Lizzy." He tilted toward her and plucked at the sheet tangled over her knees. She smelled beer and sweat and that smell of the bull.

Wheedling, coaxing. "Be a good girl, give me a kiss."

He let go of the sheet and wrapped thick fingers around the back of her neck, pulling her closer. "A little goodnight kiss, that's all, for your Cousin Joey."

Then: "Looky here, Lizzy baby, what's in my pocket? Is it money? Nah, it's better, isn't it? You could kiss it, that's what girlfriends do. You can be my girlfriend."

Despite her resolve—*don't look!*—her eyes flicked down to his other hand, fumbling with the zipper on his jeans.

Below his belly, a new bulge was protruding. In the glow of her bedside lamp, she saw it pushing out, thick and ugly.

I should scream, she thought. *Cock-a-doodle-do!*

But there's no one to hear. Pepper is deaf, he won't come.

If I close my eyes, whatever this is, it will be over faster.

But she needed to keep her eyes open and look for a chance to get away.

She kicked at him with both feet and grabbed his arm with both hands. Her chewed fingernails were useless as claws, but she tried anyway, scratching at his wrist as she bucked her body backward, bracing against the wall, kicking harder. A high, thin wail forced itself through her clenched teeth.

Joey held the back of her neck, hardly aware of her thrashing. In his lap, his other hand moved quickly, rhythmically, as he stared at her with a stupid, sick smile.

Suddenly, he released her. She scrambled into a rigid ball in the corner, pulling her knees up and tucking her head down, arms wrapped tight around her body. She wanted to turn to the wall and close off the sight of him, but she had to watch him, watch for his next move.

She heard something gasping, and something else banging—after a few seconds, she realized in a remote part of her brain that the sounds were hers. Her own breath roaring, her own heart pounding.

Joey pulled a handful of tissues from the box on her bedside table. He zipped his jeans, fastened his belt, and wadded the used tissues into a rear pocket. Swaying over her bed again, he switched off the lamp. The only light came from a pale moon, slanting through the window.

"Now it's past your bedtime," he said from the dark space above her. "You're good at keeping secrets, ain't you, Lizzy baby? We keep our secrets. Your momma and daddy won't understand, they'd be so mad if you told them about our secrets."

"You're my girlfriend now, Lizzy. My secret girlfriend. But you gotta promise you won't say nothin to your parents. They ain't gonna believe you anyway, they'll just think you're making it up. They think you're too young to be my girlfriend, but we know you're old enough, don't we?" He leaned over as if to take hold of her again. "So don't you tell them, Lizzy. Promise."

In the dark, she tasted the heat of furious tears. What choice did she have?

She whispered it. "I promise, I promise I won't tell my parents."

He nodded and turned the doorknob. He paused in the doorway, sharply backlit now from the hall light. "Nearly forgot." He swayed a little, giggling. "Nighty-night." He blew her a wet, smacking kiss. Then he closed the door and left her in the dark.

She remained curled in the corner for a long time, waiting for breath and sense to return.

When she heard her mother moving downstairs and she was sure he was gone, Liz rose and yanked the sheets off her bed, wadding them into a pile on her closet floor. Then she lay on her side under the blanket, her face to the window, feigning sleep. Knowing her mother would look in on her.

The waning gibbous moon rose high over the dark woods before she fell into a sweaty, restless sleep.

****

"Push those heels *down*, Stefanie!" Mrs. Townsend called for the umpteeth time. "Try to move *with* your horse. Post to the trot, don't bounce! Hands down, heels down! Up, down, up, down!"

Around and around Stefanie and Max trotted, wearing an uneven circular track into the grass beside the Jacobsons' big red barn. Liz leaned against the split-rail fence and frowned as she watched her friend trying to keep her balance on the little English saddle. Stephanie, so stylish in every other way, was not an elegant rider. Her arms and legs swung wildly, and her butt slapped the leather hard at every step.

Max is a saint, Liz thought, *to put up with all that bumping and flopping around.*

She didn't doubt that Mrs. Townsend knew her stuff, but this style of riding looked all wrong. At the trot, Stefanie was supposed to stand, then sit, then stand, then sit, trying to move up-down-up-down in rhythm with the pony's two-beat gait.

It was called posting, explained Mrs. Townsend, or "rising to the trot." Liz thought it would be simpler if you just sat there and tried to move *with* the bounces. Maybe without the saddle and those pesky stirrups that were swinging back and forth? Like the Comanches, they didn't use saddles.

"Okay, let's take a break. Slow down and just walk, Stefanie." Mrs. Townsend said.

Liz knew that sports coaches must have loud, clear voices to make themselves heard. A riding instructor needed an even bigger voice, to be heard across a wide field and above the noise of pounding hooves and out-of-breath riders. Mrs.

Townsend had a very loud, clear voice even though she had gray hair and was probably, like, fifty years old.

But she must be pretty worn out from coaching Stefanie, because right now she sounded out of breath and a little discouraged.

Stefanie was also breathing hard as she slid off her pony. "I think," she said to Mrs. Townsend, "it's Liz's turn. She's ridden a few times on the neighbor's horses. She can have the last fifteen minutes of my lesson time."

Liz felt her face stretch into a huge grin. What a gift this was, to be able to ride Max!

Then she glanced down in dismay, because she wasn't dressed for riding. Instead of boots and jeans, she wore only her usual sneakers and cutoffs.

Stefanie, of course, was beautifully attired in new beige jodhpurs and polished brown boots, which coordinated nicely with her Barbie-pink polo shirt. And her pink-accented riding helmet, and Max's pink saddle pad. Though right now, all that looked wet with perspiration and smeared with dust.

Mrs. Townsend hesitated. "I don't know about those shorts, Liz. The stirrup leathers will rub your legs raw. And you need boots with a heel, so your feet don't slip through the stirrups and get stuck. That's not safe."

"I can ride bareback," Liz offered. Before Mrs. Townsend could protest, Stefanie had unbuckled the girth and pulled Max's saddle off.

"And a helmet? You need a helmet." Mrs. Townsend was firm about helmets.

"Here, this will fit." Stephanie pulled off her pink helmet and shook out her blond hair. "Sorry, my helmet's yucky. I got it all gross and sweaty."

Liz merely smiled as she strapped the damp helmet on her head. Whatever was required, she'd do it—she was going to ride Max!

"Here's how you get on," Mrs. Townsend told her. "I'm going to give you a leg up. Bend your left knee and jump up from your right foot when I tell you. Try to swing your right leg over without kicking the pony." She grasped Liz's left knee and ankle with firm hands. "One, two, three."

Before Liz could say, "I don't think this will work," she was tossed up onto Max's broad back.

"Here's how you hold the reins," Mrs. Townsend was saying, "and here's where your legs should be. You can hold on with your knees but don't grab with your heels, that's a signal to go faster. Keep your shoulders back and look where you're going. Stephanie, please walk by Max's head in case he gets confused."

Liz's bare legs stuck to Max's sweaty barrel. She nudged him with her heels and he stepped forward promptly. She could feel every move he made—the swing of each step, the swell and ripple of his muscles as he walked. She was delighted by his fluid motion: the steady rise and push of his hindquarters under her seat, the lift and rotation of his shoulders in front of her knees.

"Can we trot, just a little?" Liz was really asking Max, not Stefanie.

The pony jogged forward with a steady one-two rhythm. Stefanie ran with them for a few yards and then fell behind, winded. Liz twined her fingers in Max's black mane, leaned back a little, and let the reins go slack. Whatever the pony chose to do was fine with her.

There was no jolting, no flopping, just a lovely, springy, floating motion as Max, undirected, left the circular path and trotted straight ahead into the field.

We could just keep going, Liz thought. Go faster, gallop, jump over the fence at the end. Disappear into the woods and never return.

Take me far away, Max. Please.

Max reached the end of the field and turned left, following the fence line. Slowing to a walk, he brought her back to the barn where Stefanie and Mrs. Townsend waited.

Stefanie hugged Max's neck. "You were so sweet to take such good care of Liz!" she told him. "Best pony ever!"

Mrs. Townsend looked relieved. "Liz, dear, you did very well! I can see you've ridden before—you have a natural balance. Stefanie, I'll call your mother about setting up your next lesson. Take good care of that pony, you two. He's a real treasure. 'Bye now."

Liz slid off Max. When her eyes filled with sudden tears, she ducked her head and pretended to examine the layer of dirt and pony hair that now coated the inside of her bare legs from shorts to ankles.

Stefanie said, "Mrs. Townsend said we should wash him off. I'm sure he'll just roll in the dirt after, but that's what ponies do, right?" Her pride of ownership was shining clearly as she led Max to the hose attached to the side of the barn.

"Here, I'll hold him," Stefanie told Liz. "You spray him, but do it gently. And not on his face."

Liz wiped her own face quickly on her t-shirt and held the hose reverently. She would do anything for Stefanie and Max.

She didn't quite trust her voice but she had to make the effort. "Thank you so much for letting me ride Max. You're so—generous." The words were totally inadequate. What she wanted to say was, *You just gave me the best ten minutes of my life*. But she was pretty sure Stefanie already knew that.

Stefanie laughed, a clear happy sound. "You are so welcome! You're a better rider than I am anyway. Mrs. Townsend says you're really good and she never says that about *anybody*. How did you stay on without a saddle? And how can you trot without bouncing?"

Liz shrugged. "I don't know, I just sit there."

Stefanie shook her head. "That makes zero sense. I think you're using magic. Obviously, you have it and I don't. You'll just have to help me learn your magic."

Liz nodded, not trusting her voice to get around the lump in her throat. She wasn't accustomed to hearing so much praise.

She directed the spray over Max's neck and sweaty shoulders, careful to keep the water out of his ears and nose. When he was thoroughly rinsed, she turned the water off and coiled the hose neatly, while Stefanie held the lead rope and let Max nibble grass on the lawn. Sunlight glinted off his slick, dripping body.

After a minute of grazing, Max lifted his head and stretched, stepping his front legs forward.

"Uh-oh," Stefanie said. "He's getting ready to pee. Stand back!" She scurried away, holding the very end of the lead. Liz stood near the spigot, safely out of range.

The pony's smooth dark penis slid out of its sheath and produced a torrent of acrid-smelling urine, splashing the grass and pooling in a steaming puddle.

Stefanie laughed. "Ewww! That stinks. He does it every time after a bath. My brothers can't believe how much pee a horse makes. They're so jealous."

Liz stared, chewing furiously on her lower lip, as the urine stream ended and the penis tucked itself away. Max returned to grazing.

Liz spoke as if in a trance.

"My cousin Joey took his penis out and showed it to me," she said slowly. "Last night. When I was in bed. He wanted me to—kiss it." She swallowed hard, fighting the hot tears again. "He thinks I'm going to be his—girlfriend."

Stefanie froze, eyes wide. "Oh my god. Oh Liz, that is *terrible*. What did your parents say? You've *told* them, right?"

Liz shook her head sharply as if shaking off raindrops. She dropped the hose and turned toward the barn.

"Liz, wait!" Stefanie hustled Max into his paddock and released him. She ran to the feed room and found Liz sitting on a bale of hay, staring blankly at the floor.

Stefanie grabbed Liz's hands and tugged her to her feet. "Come on. We're going to find my mother. Right *now*. You've got to tell her what you told me. We'll help you."

She placed an arm around Liz's shoulders and gently guided her toward the house, saying nothing.

***

Just before dinner, Marianna knocked tentatively on her daughter's bedroom door. Liz was sprawled on her bed, staring at an open book and gnawing on a fingernail.

"May I come in?" Her mother had never asked permission before.

Liz removed the finger from her mouth and wrapped a tissue around its bloody cuticle. She closed the book and set it in her lap, preparing herself for...whatever.

"Yes."

"I don't know how to say this." Marianna sat on the edge of the bed, right where Joey had sat the night before. She started to reach for Liz's shoulder but saw her daughter flinch, and began fussing with her own hair instead. Finger-combing and fluffing, disturbing the bright red waves that had been so carefully arranged that morning.

"I received a very upsetting phone call from Stefanie's mother this afternoon," she began. "She said that you told her—you thought that your cousin Joey was—" she stopped.

Exhaled and restarted. "That you said Joey had behaved—inappropriately." She swallowed hard. "He touched you in a bad place. And you maybe saw his—" A sharp inhale. "His privates. Yesterday. Last evening, before I got home."

Liz nodded slightly. Thinking, *Did he touch me in a bad place? He grabbed me around the neck, and the neck is not a "bad place," exactly.*

Do I have any bad places?

She'd had time to think about this. It wasn't only the touching, she wanted to explain. It was the trapping. He'd trapped her and made her watch him. And he'd wanted her to kiss him. Kiss his penis.

But okay, if it's easier for you to understand, Mom, then let's call it touching in bad places.

Marianna sat up a little straighter. "I want you to know, Elizabeth, that I've been praying about this. This is very serious, of course, so I had to pray on how to handle it. What to say to you. And your father talked to Joey. After work."

As if that mattered, not interrupting Joey at work.

"What did he say?" Liz whispered. "Joey, what did Joey say?"

"Oh, well." Her mother lifted a hand from her lap, making a small dismissive gesture. "Joey was sorry that you maybe thought that about him. He said maybe his fly was unzipped after he went to the bathroom and you saw something you shouldn't have. He thinks he was maybe careless, that way."

"What did Dad—my father—say?" Liz held her breath. A hard knot tightened in her chest and first she thought it was fear but then realized it was anger.

"Well," Marianna fumbled, "you know how men are."

No, thought Liz. The knot of anger swelled. *I'm nine, going on ten, I don't know how men are. That's your job. Tell me, please.*

"They stick together, of course," her mother continued briskly. "So who really knows the truth of it, right?"

Liz stared at this woman who claimed to be her mother. *What do you mean, who knows the truth? I do! I know the truth.*

Marianna found her confidence. "And you absolutely should have come to me first, young lady, not telling such things to Stefanie. I don't know how I'm going to deal with that—with Becky Jacobson knowing what you said about your cousin. And then she had to come to me! Why didn't you talk to me first if something made you uncomfortable?"

Not waiting for a response—clearly not wanting one—Marianna continued, "See, your father thinks you and Stefanie were just talking, the way girls do. Making up stories, and it just got a little out of hand. I know her little brothers run around naked over there, don't they? Maybe you were just thinking—"

"It wasn't *stories*. I didn't make up anything." Liz's fury simmered just below the flat surface of her words. She was no longer tongue-tied.

"It's true," she shouted. "Joey was—he had his pants open. On purpose, to show me his—penis. He had his hand on my neck so I couldn't look away. Then he was rubbing it—" She didn't have words for this part. "I don't want him here. *Ever*."

"Oh, but Elizabeth, we can't do that! We can't just banish Joey on your say-so."

Her mother's empty words landed like blows.

Is she even listening?

Marianna waved a hand dismissively. "Joey has no one else, you know that. No other family. And I have to agree with your father on this, you're much too self-conscious. Little girls have to watch what they say, not repeat what they hear from older girls who tell all those awful stories."

Liz clapped her hands over her ears and squeezed her eyes shut but her mother's voice rattled on, unstoppable.

"Terrible damage can be done," Marianna added firmly, "to a young man's reputation. To a whole family." She sighed, sounding reproachful. "I do blame myself. I shouldn't have let you go off to watch that cow being bred. I was right, you're too young for that. What was I thinking?"

Liz dropped her hands and opened her eyes to see a crimson flush flow into her mother's cheeks.

Marianna's fingers twisted in her lap. Abruptly, her voice brightened. "But we can pray together, can't we? Let's pray and ask Jesus for his help, and his forgiveness. If Jesus truly lives in your heart, you can tell him the truth and nothing can hurt you." Her mouth curled into a smile as she reached for her daughter's limp hand.

We can pray? That's it? She searched her mother's face for some way in, but saw only shutters.

Liz closed her eyes in confusion. Bowed her head out of habit, and pulled in a deep breath. "Dear Jesus," she began.

It was too weak, too small. She thought of Marianna's reverential *now-let-us-pray* voice and started over. "Jesus, help me, I beg you please as I am your humble servant."

Her mother's hand gave a squeeze. Encouraging, reassuring.

The words came to Liz from a strange new place of strength. "You can do miracles, Jesus, and that's what I need—a miracle. Please, dear Jesus, place your hand on my cousin Joey and make him see the terrible error of his ways. If that doesn't work, please strike him dead."

Marianna stiffened, clenching her daughter's hand in a sharp spasm. The pain felt good to Liz, and she gripped back as hard as she could.

Her voice rose as she opened her eyes and lifted her chin. "Deliver me now from this evil. I beg of you, dear Jesus, protect us *all* from Joey and from those who are like him. Forever and ever, thy Word be done, Amen. "

Liz remembered the other thing. "And Jesus, please tell my parents that this is not a made-up story." She caught her mother's frightened eyes and held her gaze with clear, dry eyes.

"Dear Jesus, you know that Joey sat right here where we're sitting now, and he made me promise not to tell my parents. I didn't want to break a promise so I had to tell Mrs. Jacobson first. Please, Jesus, let me know if I should go to the police because I'll do that if I have to and Mrs. Jacobson says she'll go with me. Thank you, Jesus. Amen."

Marianna shot a glance down at Liz's bed, then recoiled and snatched her hand from Liz's. She choked out a cry and stumbled to her feet. She fled then, sobbing as if she'd been abandoned in a dark forest with wild beasts lurking and all the breadcrumbs gone.

Liz let out a tight breath and picked up her phone. She wasn't supposed to use it during the dinner hour, which was now, but she expected dinner would be delayed this evening.

She sent her best friend Stefanie a text, a single line of X's and O's.

Then she picked up her book and thumbed the pages. She didn't remember her place in the story, but she knew she'd recognize it when she saw it.

Not a Burden

"What day is it?"

How many times this week has he asked that? How many times today? There's nothing wrong with his hearing. Or his memory.

I stare through green hospital curtains, out the window to a gray March sky. There's nothing there but brick walls and parking lots.

I don't have to turn around right away because I know exactly what the old man on the hospital bed looks like. He is mostly skeleton, so thin now that his elbows poke dents in the mattress. His face is gaunt. There is an ugly stubble on his chin because my mother hasn't had time to shave him.

Only the thick shock of white hair and the pale blue eyes remind me that I've known him in other places and all my life. He's a farmer, though not anymore, and his arms used to be burnt nearly black in the summer sun. He built our stone walls and plowed the fields, first with horses and then with tractors. Now his skin is as pale as the creased sheets he lies on, and nearly as dry. Cancer is turning him to cold pale wax. He is barely here, and soon he will melt entirely away.

"What day?" His voice is sharp and peevish.

"Sunday. It's still Sunday, Daddy." I turn toward him but don't meet his eyes. There's a familiar crack in the wall just over his head. I memorized it weeks ago.

"What *date?*" His voice is hoarse.

"The eighth. March eighth."

He sags back, closing his eyes. I continue to stare at the crack. Beginning at the ceiling, it wanders loosely down the wall, then widens into a deeper channel before feathering into rivulets and disappearing behind the bed. It reminds me of the river that borders our pastures, a strong wide stream where the yearling heifers and wild deer go each day for water.

On the edge of vision, I see my father's thin lips move slightly. His tongue pushes out.

I force my feet to carry me to the bedside table where an untouched lunch tray is cooling.

"Are you hungry, Daddy? You haven't eaten. You've got to eat something."

Useless words. He stopped eating a week ago. Only IV tubes feed him now, and he's tried to pull those out.

"No. Maybe tea. Just a little." His voice is whispery, nearly gone after the effort of speaking. He licks his lips without opening his eyes.

A mostly dutiful child, I uncover the little pot of hot water and unwrap a tea bag. I drop it in, careful to hang the string over the edge.

"No. It's too strong. Take it out!" He manages a near-shout and struggles feebly to grab the teabag, knocking over a glass of water on the tray. The bent straw falls to the floor and water runs off the tray.

Annoyed, I stand the glass upright and mop the tepid water with a napkin. He sinks back into the pillows but his bright pale eyes are still open, watching me. He has no apologies left to give me.

The tea bag is still in the pot. I pull it out and pour him a half cup of tea.

"Sugar?"

He shakes his head.

"Lemon? Milk?"

He waves a hand and frowns.

I place a straw in the warm, weak tea and hold it so he can drink. He sips a little then closes his lips firmly.

He looks at me, but I can't read his eyes. I don't know what he wants to tell me. Whatever it is, I don't want to hear it.

I glance away and immediately flush with shame because there on the counter is the handsome black portable radio his brother gave him. It's the best Panasonic that my uncle's 1964 dollars can buy. My parents have never had the money for such luxuries.

I covet that radio. If it were mine, I'd carry it everywhere.

What will happen to it when he dies? Will it come to me or go back to Uncle John?

Something ugly rises in my throat and I turn away.

As punishment for thinking of the radio, I drag the thought of his death forward and try it on. My father will be dead. I will have to explain to people: My father is deceased. My father passed away last week, last month, last year, forty years ago.

I indulge the small child's version of white magic: *Think of the worst, and it will not happen.*

When I was little and afraid of the dark, he would hold me in strong arms and coax me to repeat those words. *Face your fear,* he said. Imagine it, confront it, and you can manage it. Bogeymen under the bed, an owl in the pine tree, a looming shape in the closet. Stand it up, drag it out into the light, and demand an explanation.

But that only works with shadows and bedtime stories.

***

My friends at school stopped asking about my father months ago. Except for Charlene. She's not really a friend, just someone in my eighth-grade homeroom.

We could be friends but we're too cautious to make the effort. She's black, I'm white. She lives down by the railroad yard with a big noisy family; I'm an only child and I live on a dairy farm north of town. A year ago we read Nancy Drews out loud to each other at recess and this winter we were on the same basketball team, but that's about it. If we'd met when we were little kids we'd probably have become pretty good friends but now it's too hard.

On Friday morning before first period, Charlene dumped her books on her desk and said, "Hey, how's your daddy doing?"

Three other kids near us stopped talking. They looked at Charlene, looked at me, and edged away.

"Not good," I told her. "He's not eating."

The other kids drifted out into the hallway.

"I had an aunt like that," Charlene said matter-of-factly. "After her fella passed on, she just decided to die. They'd lived together nearly forever, I think. 'Don't wanna be a burden,' she told my momma. 'Don't wanna be a burden to my folks.' So she just sorta shut down and died. It was peaceful."

Charlene touched my shoulder, then dropped into her chair. "Of course, she *was* a burden because everyone fussed and tried to get her to eat, but that wasn't her fault. Maybe your daddy's like my Aunt Mabel, just doesn't wanna be a burden."

"Maybe," I said. "But he didn't lose anyone. He doesn't *need* to die. I just wish…"

She tilted her head a little and waited.

"I just wish he wasn't sick."

What I really meant was, I wish the dying man in the bed wasn't my father. My father has abandoned me. Not all at once in screams and rage and slammed doors, but a tiny bit at a time. He's slicing away the minutes, slipping off cell by cell while I sleep or listen to music or do my schoolwork. While I'm living my closed-down life.

For every minute that I forget to think of him, I lose a little more of him.

Or maybe what I wanted to say to Charlene was, *I wish I was someone else, somewhere else.*

Alone, outside this world, galloping a tall horse very fast, riding bareback on a sparkling white-sand beach. Forever.

***

My mother has returned from the ladies' room. She looks old and tired, but I know she is also strong and healthy. She takes in at a glance the wet napkin, the cup of tea, and my awkward, defiant stance. I am back at the window, staring at cars and traffic lights.

I should say something to him about how I love him. Or I should tell him the snow and ice have finally melted into mud in the cornfields. The sap ran late this year but finally the maples are pushing out those tight red buds that say SPRING. I should tell him that this morning I saw the first pointed curls of skunk cabbage poking up from the edge of the frog pond. But my voice is stuck, sinking beneath the stone in my chest.

My mother bends over the bed and smiles, murmuring words I can't hear. She smooths his hair back, clucks over the stubble on his chin, and rummages in a drawer for his electric shaver. I smell hospital soap on her hands.

"You'll be going home with Uncle John," she says without looking up. "He's in the waiting room. I'm staying here tonight. Say goodbye to your father, now."

Released, I move quickly to my father's side. Hold his hand for a moment and try to keep the relief out of my voice.

"Bye, Daddy. I'm going now."

He closes his eyes and does not speak, but his grip tightens suddenly, painfully. I resist the urge to cry out or pull away. When he finally lets go, I flee down the hall to find Uncle John.

***

We're driving home in the slush and early dusk. The clock on the dashboard of Uncle John's car glows amber and green. His new Lincoln is far finer than anything else I've ever ridden in. My parents drive the farm pickup or a crumbling Ford, older than I am.

"You know your dad's dying," Uncle John begins. A statement, not a question.

"Yeah." *Nothing new there,* I'm thinking.

"He loves you. You won't have him with you much longer. You could be a little more understanding." Uncle John must have been talking with my mom.

I want to scream but instead I lean my head against the cool window and try to listen.

My father's brother looks the way my father used to. Solid, square-shouldered, with large hands, a thick shock of gray hair, and a kind face. Uncle John is gentle, soft-spoken and generous, just as my father used to be. He's a banker, though, not a farmer. No sixteen-hour days in the hayfields for him.

I know enough to realize I'm insolent with him because I wish we had more money, like him. Also, he doesn't have cancer and he isn't dying.

I say the first bitter thing that comes into my head. "He'd be okay if he'd just eat. He's given up. He doesn't even *try* to get well." It's his own fault, I mean. He could get better if he really wanted to. If he loved me enough.

"Food tastes pretty awful when you're on those drugs," Uncle John says mildly. "Maybe you wouldn't know about that."

"No, I guess not." I am suddenly very tired. My face is wet from the condensation on the window or something else.

We're both silent for a few minutes. Heading home to a silent empty house, I watch the cold faraway lights of other people's houses swing by. Then we've left behind the lights and the neat tidy houses. We drive through a dark forest where there's nothing but wilderness stretched out beneath the invisible new moon. I imagine white-tailed deer and black bears watching from beneath the oaks. They can see us in the glow of the dashboard but we will never see them.

"You know," Uncle John says quietly, "your daddy wishes he'd been a better father to you."

Caught in self-pity, I straighten up. A slow heat spreads up my neck.

He says, "Farmers don't make much money. I don't have to tell you that. Your dad's a farmer because he loves it. He believes that working the land and loving his family are the most important things anybody can do. But he wishes he could've given you more of the things you want. Clothes, a new TV, your own portable radio."

I think, *Is it that obvious?* Tears threaten but I'm too tough to cry.

Uncle John continues, "He hasn't been able to do much that way. And now his time's up. There's just one more thing he can do to help your mom and you. There's some insurance money. Not a lot, but still something. It's a term policy. You know how that works? If a person dies before a specified date, it pays out. After that date, it expires and isn't worth anything."

Anger lodges in my throat again. *Wow. My dad's dying and my uncle's giving me a lecture on insurance. Go to hell, Uncle John.*

He keeps talking. "That policy expires on the fifteenth. He told me it's like a wall he's got to climb over by that date. Today's the eighth, so he's got seven days. If he lives longer than seven days, there's no money for you and your mom."

He pauses. Adds, "I think he'll make it in time. Extraordinary, isn't it? What we do for love."

There is no air in the car, no light in the streets. This place I occupy becomes a great hole and I've fallen in.

Gasping for breath, tumbling through a wilderness of space, I'm clutching a small silent radio hard to my chest. There's no trail back, no path forward. The thing I'm carrying is too heavy and there's no place to set it down.

WITNESSING

The skinny preacher calls it witnessing, but really it's sin-bragging. Boasting and shaming, all bundled up in one big weepy mess.

"We shall witness your submission to Jesus as you confess your sins! You will be washed in the blood of the lamb!"

Ooh, a metaphor. My eighth-grade English teacher loves metaphors.

Aunt Ruthie's current preacher-crush is sermonizing about how we can get healed through witnessing. Because Jesus died in full public view on Calvary, Peacher Duval is telling us we all should confess our sins. Loudly, in front of a thousand strangers.

Aunt Ruthie and Mom and me are sitting in row six, guaranteed premium seats. My aunt leans over my mother to assure me *everyone* will be witnessing tonight, so we shouldn't feel singled out. Ruthie's so excited she's practically levitating, blue eyes tilted heavenward.

Up on stage, Preacher Duval is twisting himself around like he's channeling Mick Jagger in an old YouTube video. His shiny pink shirt has sweaty pits. Black sequins on the chest spell out JESUS LOVES ME!

More yelling. "Jesus knows your pain *and* your sins! You must *stand up* for him! Witness, and be cleansed!"

The old field house vibrates as chairs get shoved around and boots thump the wooden floor. Ruthie leaps to her feet with the rest of the crowd. "Get up, you two!" she yells at Mom and me.

I glance at Mom. She frowns at me, then scowls at her older sister.

Duval screams, "Will you stand up?"

Ruthie and the crowd bellow, "Yes, Lord!"

Mom touches my arm and whispers. "Sam. Y'all feel a need to stand up?"

"Um, no. This is weird. Can we leave?"

"That'd be awkward, since Ruthie drove us." Mom settles back and crosses her arms, looking like she's prepared to sit there all night. "We can wait it out. Think about something nice."

It's too noisy for thinking. Tambourines clatter, trumpets blare. An invisible choir belts out a hymn I don't know as Duval stretches his arms overhead, eyes closed. A thousand people begin swaying and calling out their sins to each other. Many are shouting, like they think Jesus is deaf.

A bushy-bearded man grips the chair in front of him. "That pickup I sold! The transmission was shot, I knew it. But I took the kid's money anyway."

"I sinned, too!" a red-faced woman shouts. "I cheated on my taxes!"

A red-faced man pats her shoulder. "Nah, doesn't count."

"I had sex with the plumber!" a bottle-blonde woman cries. "Twice!"

Another woman hugs her and shouts, "Praise the Lord!"

I turn to Mom. "Seriously. *Why* are we here?"

She just shakes her head. We're in the middle of a sea of sobbing sinners but she's just sitting there, all cool and detached. I want to be cool too but my ponytail's too tight. I yank off the elastic and finger-comb a hair curtain around my face. Wishing I'd worn a hoodie so I could pull myself in like a turtle.

Except for a few ancients in wheelchairs, Mom and me are the only people still sitting. Duval's scanning the hall now, probably looking for us sitters. He jumps off the stage and I lose sight for a moment in the crowd but I know he's coming because the spotlight's tracking him.

"We're just going to watch," Mom told Aunt Ruthie earlier that evening. "We'll listen to the sermon and sing a hymn, if it's one we know."

Aunt Ruthie should've explained it all right then. Should've said, you can't go to a revival meeting and just sit there.

Duval's found us. He's pretty young, mid-twenties maybe. Lots younger than the Unitarian minister, Reverend Allenby, who used to take Dad fishing for black drum out on the Albermarle. Dad promised he'd take me too, someday, but then he got sick.

The preacher's wearing black jeans and a wide belt with a trophy buckle the size of a hatchet blade. What the rodeo kids call a belly platter, but this one has a rhinestone cross where a bucking bronc should be. That belt buckle is right at eye-level and closing in fast.

I feel his hand clutch the back of my chair.

Mom stiffens and side-eyes me. "Stay in your seat, Sam."

Then he's gone again. The crowd closes around us and the confessing ramps up again.

My aunt, on the far side of Mom, shoots stink eye at us between cries of *Hallelujah!* and *Praise the Lord!* Her cheeks are bright pink, a match for her smeared lipstick, and her polyester rose-patterned dress is sticking to her thighs. Too bad cellphones are banned because it'd be cool to shoot Aunt Ruthie right then.

It would serve her right. My mother's bible-clutching sister started burying her nose closer into our lives about five months ago, just before Dad died. Mom's working double shifts now at the Super Walmart so mostly it's me that Ruthie sees when she "just stops by" in the afternoons. Whenever I hear her old Ford thumping down our dirt road, I hide.

Last Monday when I got off the bus she was already there, pawing through the recycle bin outside the kitchen door. She asked me how much wine Mom was drinking and muttered something about "an intervention."

That evening she talked Mom into taking a night off so we three could attend this revival meeting, led by this evangelist who would quote-unquote "assist with moving you forward to your acceptance of grief."

Apparently, we're stuck on the wrong level of sorrowing.

Mom's got plenty on her plate right now, like hospital bills.

When I get home from school every day, she's just starting her evening shift at Wally-world, so she needs me to do for myself each evening. Eat, shower, do your homework, stay out of trouble. Which I'm doing, mostly, though my science grades slipped a bit for a while. For a few months, I wasn't really seeing the point of science.

Mom and me, we're coping. We get where we need to be, do what we need to do. The wine is her business.

But the grief-stage failure and Mom's drinking aren't the only reasons Aunt Ruthie drove us five hours round-trip through the mountains to find salvation at the feet of Preacher Duval.

Apparently, I'm heading right down the path to damnation.

About two weeks ago, Ruthie called Mom at work to report the emergency of me doing something very sinful with a boy in our back yard. Mom promised she'd talk to me but we haven't had five minutes alone together to discuss anything. Then Ruthie convinced Mom this revival meeting would be good for us, so here we are. Exhibit A.

Instead of pulling that thread any further, I'd rather think about Davey, my best friend. He likes to draw and plans to be a doctor, so he always carries a box of fine-tip markers and a body-parts coloring book in his backpack. If Davey was here tonight, he'd be explaining sweat glands and vocal cords, or sketching ears and noses.

There's a sudden clash of cymbals.

"Time for the healing," Ruthie shout-whispers.

Organ music swells and fades as the preacher and a dozen others appear on stage. They all form a line, holding hands. A sad-looking woman cutches Duval's forearm.

The stage lights dim to amber, a poor choice. It makes everyone look ill and I remember my father's skin turning yellow before doctors removed his gall bladder. Jaundice, Davey explained.

The people on stage pass the microphone, witnessing their miracles. All have been healed of something—

epilepsy, MS, breast cancer. *Thank you Jesus!* they say, and the crowd roars a collective *Hallelujah!*

Pushing damp curls off her forehead, Ruthie nudges Mom. "See, what'd I tell you. It works."

Mom stares straight ahead, her mouth a tight line.

Ruthie tugs at her skirt, failing to straighten it over her knees. "Pastor Duval was here last year. Y'all should've come here then. Your Jonathan would still be with us."

She glances over. "Samantha, you're doing that thing, pushing your mouth in. Don't twist your face up like that, it's ugly."

Mom lifts an eyebrow at me. My face goes hot because I didn't know I was doing it, chewing the flesh inside my cheek. It started when Dad was in the hospital. When he couldn't talk, and I couldn't think of anything to say.

The familiar taste rises like red salt and copper. Swallowing, I wipe a quick finger around my mouth, then sit on my hands so they'll behave.

The music soars triumphant, a victory hymn. I can't help fidgeting, tasting blood again.

Blood should stay beneath the skin along with the organs, all working together. The liver, paired with the pancreas. Davey explained the pancreas, a curved blob about six inches long behind the stomach.

The eight months my father was sick, I never said the c-word. But after the funeral, I saw his death certificate and autopsy report. Then I wanted to know *everything* about cancer.

Two weeks after my father's death, I was sitting with Davey on the bank behind our cowbarn.

—What's a pancras?

—It's pan-cre-as, not pan-cras. It helps with digestion. Makes insulin to control sugar levels in the blood.

—My dad had diabetes. They should've tested for cancer, too.

—Lots of things can go wrong with the pancreas. Cancer is rare but it's really hard to treat. They have to catch it quick.

I tucked my head down against Davey's shoulder so he wouldn't see me cry, then I stayed there because his shoulder felt almost as good as my dad's.

The noise of scraped chairs yanks me back into the field house. People are turning their chairs to face us, forming a rough circle with us in the center. They rise to their feet, murmuring and staring.

I scoot my chair closer to Mom and widen my eyes in that way you do to alert someone to danger. This is beyond cringey—it's gone straight into weird.

The preacher bellows suddenly, "The power of *all* these true believers shall raise you up!" He's right behind us and his voice sounds wet, like he's fighting phlegm. "We will all *help* you to stand! Up! Through the love! Of Jesus! *You. Will. Be. Saved!*"

People shuffles closer, arms outstretched. Trapping us, imploring us to rise. Panic mixes with the blood in my mouth and I want to scream, but there's no air.

The crowd parts and he closes in.

Mom grabs my shoulder, snagging a fold of shirt like I'm a kid about to get run over. Her nostrils flare but she stays planted on that hard metal chair like an oak tree's roots holding onto granite. I want to be awesome and magnificent like her so I sit up straight and stare at the only thing I can see, the front of the preacher's neon-pink shirt.

My eyes are even with his ribcage, about where his gall bladder would be.

—Where does a surgeon start? I'd asked Davey. What happens first?

—You locate the gall bladder and draw an outline on the skin.

—What comes next?

—Take your scalpel and make the first cut. Fold back the skin, clamp the blood vessels with hemostats. When you can slip your fingers in below the lowest rib, feel for the gall bladder.

I could do that to Preacher Duval, that's how close he's standing.

Everything goes suddenly quieter as people turn to find their seats. Now we're all sitting, except for Duval.

He crouches, anchoring himself with one hand on the back of my chair, and brings his face tight in to mine. He's got greasy-looking black hair and mud-green eyes, what Davey would call military green. The microphone dangles in his free hand and he's breathing hard, exhaling something rancid and sour. He aims a conspirator's voice at Mom and me.

"If you don't feel ready yet, I can help you." His voice is low, a hollow-sounding confidence.

I curl away from his sour breath.

"I know it's hard," he urges us in that low voice, "when someone you love has passed into the arms of Jesus. Jonathan, right? Your loving husband, your loving father. But God had other plans for Jonathan. You must find your own salvation and you do that by giving *everything* to Jesus.

"Just step through that door," he coaxes. "Just the two of you, and me, with Jesus. Come through the door." He waves a hand and I realize he's pointing to a real door at the far side of the hall.

I think I've figured it out. We make him look bad, Mom and me. Everybody else stands, sits, moves on command, cries and sings to the script. But we're threatening him with our silence and our sitting.

If we walk through that door, the threat of us will vanish. We will vanish.

Mom stares straight ahead, planted on her chair. The preacher keeps squatting beside me, mouth-breathing his smelly air.

Ruthie fusses and quivers beside us. The rest of the congregation holds its breath.

It's Duval who breaks.

"Dammit." His voice is half-snarl, half-whisper. "What the *fuck* are you doing here in my church if you're not gonna declare yourselves *saved*?"

A silent *Hallelujah* pops into my brain, because that single word—that *fuck*—will break this logjam. He's just pulled Mom's trigger.

My mother never swears. And she won't tolerate anyone who does.

Mom turns, spears Preacher Duval's cloudy green eyes with her own dark brown ones, and clears her throat. She's readying her assistant manager's voice, the one that carries all the way across Wally-world's Women's Plus, beyond Housewares, and right up front into Produce.

In this collective hush, she doesn't need a microphone.

"Reverend," she says crisply, "bless your anxious heart. My daughter and I have made a mistake. We've obviously come to the wrong place. We'll save you further aggravation now by leaving. Samantha, let's go."

He's still crouching beside me, looking confused and angry but not moving fast enough. As she rises, she places a hand on his pink-shirt shoulder and gives a gentle shove, just enough to unbalance him. He sprawls hard on the dirty floor, grunting when he smacks an elbow.

The crowd gasps but Mom just grabs my hand, pulling me up and out of my sixth-row premium seat. Now that everyone else in that packed hall is sitting down or fallen flat on the floor, the two of us are up on our feet, walking out.

Escaping.

Liberation makes me giddy, but I move calmly beside my mother, out through the double doors flung wide to the soft May night. Then I let go her hand and sprint past all the cars into a hayfield beyond the parking lot. Mom's right behind me.

The night air is warm, fragrant with fresh-cut hay, and above us is the light of a billion stars. There's a crescent moon hanging overhead.

We find two big rocks covered with lichen and sit, facing the field. Catching our breath and watching fireflies flash their strobe lights and listening to the rattle of crickets and cicadas.

My mother sighs. "Sam, I'm sorry we got pulled into that circus. Shall we just chalk it up to experience? Sort of an experiment." She rubs the back of her neck. "Ruthie had me convinced it would be good for us."

"It's okay, we survived."

"We did." A pause. "But we still need to talk, you and me."

"Okay."

"Me first. My—" She looks away at the woods beyond the field. "My drinking."

Not what I'd expected. "Umm—it's okay, Mom. I get it, you need to relax. Get the job out of your head."

"No, it's not okay. And I shouldn't be spending our money on wine. So, I'm done."

"You can do that? Just stop?"

"I think so." She squares her shoulders. "Yes, I can. I will. It'll be worth it to see the look on Ruthie's face when I tell her I've quit drinking without her help."

"She'll take credit anyway. The power of prayer."

Mom laughs, a light clear sound I haven't heard in months. "I'm sure she will."

"So I don't have to hide the empty bottles anymore."

"Oh." She shoots me a glance. "You've been doing that?"

"When I thought Ruthie was coming by."

"I'm sorry. You shouldn't have to do that." She wipes her eyes with a hand and tilts her head up. "Look, we can see the Milky Way. I've never seen Arcturus so bright."

"Where?"

"You know. See the Big Dipper?" She points. "Look for Polaris, the North Star. Like Dad taught us."

"Polaris, right, found it. Then Arc to Arcturus, spike to Spica."

"Yes. Your father loved the night sky, didn't he?"

I nod, feeling a familiar choke in my throat. But it's not so bad out here, under the stars.

Then I wait, because she needs to ask me.

"So, Sam. About Davey. You're thirteen—"

"Nearly fourteen."

"—and he's sixteen. Ruthie says she saw you and Davey doing something she thought was sinful, but she wouldn't say what."

"Aunt Ruth sees sin everywhere. She's wrong—"

"I'm not relying on her words. I'd like you to tell me yourself."

"So that's why she dragged us here tonight. It's *my* fault?" I say it too sharp and need to walk it back. Mom doesn't need my shit on top of hers.

I try again. "Remember how Davey helped me get caught up at school, back in March?"

"After the funeral."

"Yeah." I taste blood again, stale like old sourdough, and swallow hard. "Everyone was avoiding me at school. Even the teachers tippy-toed around. No one wanted to hear me talk about Dad, except Davey. He was cool."

"He wants to be a doctor, right?"

"A surgeon. So he researched the cancer, to help me understand why Dad died."

"Oh, Sam. There's no 'why.' It just—happened."

"But there's a medical reason, right?"

"Oh—I see. Not that kind of a why. More of a what."

I quit gnawing on my lower lip. The words will drown in blood if I don't get them out fast.

"So I kind of owed him, see? For helping."

"And?"

"There's this other thing. Everybody thinks Davey's gay because he's smart and nerdy, not a jock. He needed to say he'd kissed a girl, to stop the bullying. I'd be his proof, see? His witness."

I drop my hands to the rock I'm sitting on and shift a little, trying to get comfortable. The rock's coat of lichen feels like rubber beneath my hands. I pick off a bit and roll it between my palms. It's a stretchy peel, cool and elastic like a fold of skin. The skin of the rock.

Low clouds drift above, blurring the shape of the crescent moon. I squint and it becomes the curl of a pancreas.

—Where is it? I'd asked Davey. Show me my pancreas. Draw it.

I pulled my shirt up and held the skin taut. With a thin purple marker, he traced the curve on my abdomen.

—Purple, he said. Cancer is like a terrible purple flower.

—Where's my gall bladder? Make it yellow, like jaundice. Label it.

—That's next to your liver. Green for the liver.

—And my heart?

—Red, of course. But your shirt's in the way.

So I pulled it off.

With infinite care, Davey helped me understand what I was made of, blood and bones and sorrow and love.

That night, gazing into the mirror, I was astonished by the marvelous bouquet blooming on my skin in crimson, scarlet, emerald, indigo, violet, gold. All the parts of me I'd never seen, now forever illuminated.

"And then?" My mother's face is a dark silhouette under the pancreas moon. "What you said about Davey, him asking you to be his witness. What happened then?"

"I kissed him. Once."

"That's it, one kiss?"

"One kiss. No big deal."

A Friend Next Door

Everything wants rain but there's none coming today, Aunt Lena says. She's the one in charge of declaring things so it's gotta be true.

I say yeah my garden needs rain, but then all this stupid dust would just change itself to slick red mud. The rain would probably come in too heavy and we'd surely get flooded out again. Then it's outta the trailer and back to a Red Cross shelter.

Aunt Lena gives me her sideview stink-eye, the look that means I'm working too hard on my smartass smirk. She pushes her head farther down into the bush beans and mutters something about ungrateful girls dissing their elders.

Most times she's right about the weather, but I'm feeling mean so I want to remind her she's so big and rickety she can't stand upright without pulling on something to get up off her knees. Sometimes it's me, the thing she hauls up on. Today it's the sharp-edged steel T-post at the corner of my garden, a rusted stake holding up bits of sagging chicken wire that's supposed to keep rabbits and whistle-pigs out. Nothing here is sturdy enough for serious leaning-on.

Aunt Lena drags herself upright and drops an apronful of vegetables into her old gather-basket. A dozen okras, two shriveled-up cucumbers, and a pocketful of withered snap beans with all the snap gone.

She smacks her big gloves together to bump off the dirt and get my attention. Those were Daddy's gloves but Lena says anything he left behind is ours now so she wears them to protect her fancy nails when she goes in the garden. Which isn't very often. It's my garden and I'm the one who digs in the dirt and pulls weeds. I don't have gloves, I have calluses and broken nails that the dirt never comes out from under.

I know Lena's waiting on me to look up so she can say something more but I'm still down here in the dust, searching through vines and nutsedge for any tomatoes that the kingbirds haven't pecked holes in. I figure she'll say her piece whether I look at her or not.

She pushes a coil of gray hair back under her navy visor. This visor's Ralph Lauren, she says. From the twenty-sixteen US Open. That's tennis.

Like I might've not known it's tennis, like she hasn't said it a gazillion times. The first time being right after she found that stupid visor at Goodwill. It's faded and stained with somebody else's sweat but hey, it's a Ralph Lauren. It has the word RALPH stitched big across the front so everyone at the Dollar General thinks my aunt's name is Ralph. She insists it's a good conversation starter, and that's important if you want to get a job in retail. Which she does.

I pretend I can't hear her say her piece about the visor and I almost can't anyway because the backhoes and bulldozers and dump trucks are making their godawful racket in the lot next door. It's a blasting clanging pounding that grits your teeth and grinds right into your brain.

I complain about the noise. Lena reminds me those are *con*-struction machines, not *dee*-struction. *Con*-struction means progress.

That's not progress, it's the sound of violence. It's machine monsters ripping the earth apart into a red grime that rises up and falls on everything in my garden, the okra and corn and cukes. All the stuff I'm trying to sell so I can get a couple shirts and a new pair of jeans for sixth grade.

I don't have many customers. Most of our neighbors avoid this road because of the *con*-struction traffic. Last evening, a dump truck driver stopped for a few ears of corn and a couple tomatoes, and Mr. Billings always buys something when he comes by each Friday to collect the rent money for our trailer. But that's it, customer-wise.

The dirt blew in so bad last week, Mama gave me an old sheet to drape over the card table that I use for a vegetable stand. The sheet keeps the dust off, but it doesn't help the stink of grease and diesel and tar hanging in the air.

Aunt Lena says that's just the smell of our good fortune about to land. There's a new strip mall going in next door, with a CVS, a Chik-Fil-A, and her favorite, a nail salon. And a big asphalt parking lot. Maybe someday, praise the lord, even a Walmart. Those're all gonna be our new neighbors, my aunt says. Our new friends.

I'm pretty sure I don't have any friends. We've moved five times in two years and I'm not expecting much from this new school, either.

Most afternoons when Mama's back from her shift at the cleaners and the sun is slanting down through the sweetgums in the sideyard, we carry our glasses of sweet tea out to the not-rotten part of our deck, to watch the construction next door. Lena always takes the lawn chair so Mama and I sit on the porch steps, or on stood-up chunks of firewood that we won't need until November.

Mama and Lena smooth out paper towels on their laps, like pressed linen napkins. Lena sips her tea all ladylike and gossips about people I don't know.

Mostly I sit and pick at the greeny-gray mold on the plastic siding of our single-wide. I could go inside but it's not any cooler in there and really I'm hoping to spot some of the construction workers with their shirts off. The men all wear filthy jeans and worn-out boots. By the end of a hot sticky day some have pulled off their raggedy t-shirts. They soak their heads and shoulders under a water spigot to keep going in the heat.

The men don't know I'm spying on them back here, beyond their trenches and culvert pipes and mountains of dirt. If I sit at just the right angle and squint through the sweetgums, I can see their bare wet shoulders and broad backs, their muscled arms swinging shovels and pickaxes. They are burnt dark and dirty with sun and sweat and grit.

Seeing those shirtless men doesn't balance out the hateful noise, the dust and the diesel fumes, but they are something to think about.

Lena sips her tea and declares that CVS'll start hiring soon. Later this month or, for sure, the month after, so they'll have everyone trained up by the time it's ready to open. She says she's positioned herself real good, living so close 'cause she can just walk over next door and boom, there she'll be, on time for every shift. She knows their whole hairproducts line and all their cosmetologies. She saves all the CVS circulars that come in the mail, with the ads and discounts. She's got it all memorized, so they'll have to hire her, right? She'll be first one in the door, right at the top of their hiring list.

Lena slaps the arm of the lawn chair and grins. I want to tell her not to smile so big because people won't want to see those missing teeth. But I stay quiet. I'm not really listening anyway because I'm watching one of the men shovel pea gravel into a nearby culvert. He looks maybe a few years older than me, slim and brown and easy in his movements, swinging the shovel with steady strength. Though it's the end of the workday so he must be hot and tired. I could make him a glass of sweet tea. Strong and sugary with extra ice so the glass drips heavy with sweat and gets all slippery.

Mama doesn't ever say much. She's always tired from working at the cleaners and I know she worries about Mr. Billings maybe wanting to sell the land our home sits on. She misses Daddy and so do I, but I don't know what to do about any of that so I just watch the men working.

Aunt Lena finishes her sweet tea. She reminds me again when that CVS comes in, it'll be just like having a new friend.

"Book. Lamp. Table." The homecare nurse enunciates carefully, her easy Carolina drawl opening the vowels and turning *lamp* into *lay-ump*. Her dark eyes narrow slightly with the effort to be precise and professional.

"Book, lamp, table," she repeats. Her name is Charmaine, accent on the first syllable. Charmaine is tall, angular, and dark-skinned with tight black hair woven into intricate cornrows. She's sitting at the small kitchen table in Edith Mullen's cluttered apartment, surrounded by nice antiques and stacks of junk mail.

Across the table, Edith settles her considerable 91-year-old backside firmly into the seat of her red-cushioned wheelchair. She hunches forward, resting ancient forearms on the table's stained burlwood. Her thin lips, startlingly pink and a little crooked, silently mouth the same three words.

They lock eyes and lean toward each other over the small table: the slender young black woman in her crisp blue nurse's scrubs and the wizened old white woman in her pink polyester pantsuit.

Behind them, Edith's younger sister Jenna is propped against the kitchen counter. She's dressed in baggy jeans, sandals, and a worn t-shirt. A single plume of silver ponytail, wrenched back and bound with a rubber band, hangs on her neck. Jenna crosses her bare ankles and keeps an eye on the old table, ready to leap into action if its fold-out leaves give way.

A shaft of thin sunlight slants from the narrow window across the room. Charmaine squints a little in the dusty light, then smiles encouragingly. "You can remember those three words, right, Miz Edith? I'll ask you to say them again in a few minutes. It's a little memory game, helps me figure out how you're doing, all right? Book, lamp, table."

Edith's wispy, over-permed white hair flutters a little in the ceiling fan's sluggish breeze. She forms the words again, practicing silently before saying them out loud. "Book. Lamp. Table." Pausing after each word and attempting to copy Charmaine's southern inflection.

Then she abandons the fake drawl and shouts, "Book! Lamp! Table!" Delighted, she slaps the tabletop sharply with both palms, making it vibrate. "Got it! Like a BLT! Book, lamp, table!"

Startled, Charmaine jerks back a little. "Very good, Miz Edith." She lifts slim manicured hands, palms outward, as if calming a manic puppy.

Jenna pushes herself off the counter and crouches to inspect the underside of the old table. It's a family heirloom, not designed for enthusiasm. She checks the leaf braces and repositions a wobble-correcting napkin wedged under one foot.

The nurse ignores me. "Just a few more questions, Miz Edith. Can you tell me a little about your parents? When was your momma born? And where, do you know that?"

Edith pats her flown-away hair and launches into a story. "Oh, our mother's name was Villa, rhymes with Willa but starts with a V. I bet you've never heard that one before. Isn't that so pretty? It means a grand house in Spanish, because her grandfather was a sea captain and he sailed all over, so to speak, down to places like South America, and his ship was named…"

"The *Villa Maria.*" Jenna crawls out from beneath the table, stretches a kink out of her back, and returns to her place by the sink.

"Edie," she adds, "can you please just answer the questions? Charmaine asked you when Mother was born. And where."

"I was getting there," Edith snaps. "And she asked *me*, not you. There's nothing wrong with my hearing. The ship was named the *Villa Maria.* April 23, 1909, she was born, but I don't know where. They all traveled a lot. And there were so many of them. All over."

"Mother was one of twelve children," Jenna offers. "We actually aren't sure where Mom was born. The family bible had her birth date but not the location. Somewhere in Vermont or Massachusetts, I'd guess, or maybe Nova Scotia where Grandpa was from."

Charmaine looks from Edith to Jenna. "Thank you, Miz Jenna, but I need Miz Edith to tell me what she can recall." Jenna shrugs in apology. Thinking: *Okay, you can sort out the next pronoun storm on your own.*

Edith shoots a dark look at her younger sister. "It was somewhere they speak French, I know that. She spoke French. Though she had that Spanish name. But she learned that in school, the French. She was very smart, so to speak."

Charmaine looks confused but she presses on. "Miz Edith, was your mother Hispanic?"

"No, good heavens, of course not," Edith shakes her head emphatically. "I have blue eyes, see? We all do. She was from Vermont."

"Okay. And when did your momma pass?"

"Oh, yes!" Edith smiles broadly, showing a mouth of yellow dentures. "Mother was so smart, she was brilliant. She passed all her classes early and then she skipped two grades, went right into high school. That's why he thought she was so much older. But then she met him and got married and never graduated high school. So to speak."

Charmaine looks lost and Jenna has to translate again. "Edie, Miz Charmaine asked about when Mother *passed on*, not when she passed her classes or why Dad thought she was older. The question is, when she died." She pushes a jumbled stack of magazines and catalogs off the second kitchen chair and sits beside her sister's wheelchair.

"Oh, well, then," Edith frowns. "She should've said so. Still, she was that smart, like I said. But she died in 1964."

Jenna suppresses a sigh. "No, Edie, Dad died in 1964, Mother in 1984."

Charmaine tries to recover control. "Miz Jenna, please, I need Miz Edith to say it."

Edith scowls at Jenna, then says, "It was a long time ago. Daddy died so young, when he was only 64. We kids were all in our late thirties when Daddy died."

Jenna shakes her head. "No, Edie, I was in eighth grade. *You* were thirty-six when Dad died, but I was only thirteen."

Edith and Charmaine both stare at Jenna.

"No," Edith said, "That can't be right. Jenna, you were in college, I know that. And pregnant." She scowls and thumps the table with a closed fist for emphasis.

"No." Jenna sighs. "I was thirteen. Not pregnant."

Charmaine abandons her script and turns to Jenna. "You're *how* many years younger than Miz Edith?"

"Twenty-three years. Mom got married at 15, Dad was 24." Jenna is hoping to get through this detour quickly. They're already a half-hour late for lunch. "Mom had four kids by the time she was 20. Twenty-one years later, she had me. Same parents, same farmhouse, same high school, even the same art teacher. I had two brothers and two sisters, but they were all grown and gone by then. Edith was third of those four, I'm number five. Now everyone else is gone. Edith and I are the only ones left."

Not the whole story, Jenna thinks, but it's all you need. And why does it matter?

The longer version would include more details, like the part about Mom getting pregnant a month after her fifteenth birthday by a man almost ten years older. There was always the question of who had seduced whom, back in 1924 when respectable young women absolutely did not have sex before marriage.

"So…if Miz Edith is ninety-one, you're… sixty-eight?" Charmaine stares at Jenna.

Edith looks blank. Jenna nods. "Yeah. I'm the age Dad would have been when his youngest daughter—that's me— graduated high school. If he'd lived."

"But she's talking to *me*," Edith interjects sharply. "This is *my* story. And the best part is this! Now my baby sister has moved near me, and now we are getting to know each other. And I'm just tickled to death. Like that song Eliza sang."

Charmaine is lost again. "Eliza?"

"She's thinking Eliza Doolittle," Jenna explains. "But really it's Anna who signs it. From that musical? *The King and I.*"

The nurse just shakes her head.

Edith flashes her open-mouthed smile, lifts her head and begins trilling in an off-key soprano, "Getting to know you, getting to know all about you…"

She breaks off singing and adds triumphantly, "See, now I get to learn all about my little baby sister. All about her, everything I missed before. And she's learning everything about me!"

Oh, Edie, Jenna thinks, *you can't know. You simply weren't there. So no, you can't know me. And whatever you do know, you don't approve of.*

Jenna keeps her voice pleasant. "I always thought that song was creepy. No one can know all about anyone."

Edith's winning smile flattens into a scowl. Abruptly, she leans forward, reaching for Jenna's ponytail with a gnarled hand. Jenna is ready for the move. She tilts her chair back and remains just out of reach.

"Jenna," Edith scolds, "you mustn't ever pull your hair back behind your ears like that. Ears are ugly, they detract from your face. Where are your earrings? Ladies wear earrings, and they hide their ears with their hair so the ugly parts stay covered up. You need a proper haircut. Comb your hair forward to cover your ears and spray it in place. A permanent would help. Or you could just wear one of my wigs, that would look nice. While we're on the topic, so to speak, your pants are baggy—"

"No, thank you," Jenna looks away, tamping down the need to lash back. "I like my jeans. And I like my hair the way it is. So to speak."

She glances pointedly at the clock over the kitchen sink and says to Charmaine, "Sorry. We don't want to miss our lunch."

The nurse's eyebrows have risen almost into her neatly braided hair. Caught in a battle she can't possibly understand, she chooses strategic retreat. She pats Edith's hand reassuringly and gathers her paperwork, then pushes back her chair and looks for the door.

"You have such interesting stories, Miz Edith," Charmaine says briskly, "and you must be so happy to have your baby sister here, now, where she can visit and help you like she does. Thank you, I do believe I'm about done."

Edith fixes her sociable face into place, preparing to be gracious with her goodbyes.

Charmaine closes her notebook, zips the blood pressure cuff into its case, and stands. "Tomorrow I'll write up my report. The office will get back to you real soon on your homecare claim, Miz Edith. Then we can set up that extra help you're needing. For bathing and dressing, housework and such. I know Miz Jenna comes a couple days a week, but she can't do everything. You need more help, every day.

"One last question, Miz Edith. Do you remember those three words I asked you to memorize?"

Edith stares up at Charmaine, mouth open and trembling. "What words? I know the Lord's Prayer. Those words? 'Our Father who art—'"

"Those three words we worked on memorizing, earlier."

Edith looks to her sister, hoping for help but finding none. She closes her eyes tightly and twists her gnarled hands together on the table.

"Chair," she says. Desperation creeps in. "No, no, not chair. Lamp. Lamp and paper. Book? Yes, book! BLP? No, no, can't eat that. Paper's wrong."

The old woman sits in frustrated silence. Angry, defeated, unable to capture the third word from the stew of memory.

"That's okay, Miz Edith," Charmaine pats her shoulder reassuringly. "You did real good. You got two out of three, that's good."

The caseworker gathers her jacket and case and gives Jenna a sympathetic nod. She closes the apartment door gently behind her.

Furious, Edith spins her wheelchair back from the table and glares at Jenna. "That woman tricked me!" she shouts. "I remembered everything just fine until she distracted me, we were having a nice chat, I thought we were done, and then she did that to me when I thought we were all finished! That's what she did, she tricked me! And you were no help whatsoever!"

Jenna sighs and stands. "She was just doing her job, Edie, not trying to trick you. I wasn't supposed to help. Here, I'm putting together a sandwich. You want ham and cheese or chicken salad with lettuce-tomato?"

As Jenna expects, the question of food catches Edith's attention. "Chicken! I love chicken salad." Just like that, the anger is gone, swamped beneath a new confetti storm of memory fragments. "Mom made the best chicken salad. And roast chicken on Sundays, too, didn't she? I remember all the chickens we had on the farm when we were kids. We traded eggs to other people. Even traded a dozen chickens for a goat, once. I liked gathering eggs, but I didn't like the chickens. Stupid, smelly things. Especially in the summer when it rains because the chicken coop gets so stinky. Daddy always made the boys clean it out. They hated that. Remember?"

Jenna is poking through the refrigerator. She finds mayonnaise, days-old white bread, a cooked chicken breast, limp lettuce, no tomatoes. She makes a mental note to give the fridge a good cleaning, then locates a dull knife and a small cutting board. She begins shredding chicken.

"Remember? About the chickens?" Edith insists.

"No, Edie." Jenna suppresses a sigh. "Not really. The chickens got sold when I was four. What you're talking about, that was twenty years earlier. But speaking of chickens I do remember the story that Mother always told me about your wedding."

"What story? Was it a funny story?" Edith tips her head to one side.

Jenna is struck by her elderly sister's resemblance to a bright-eyed broody hen. Age has pulled the skin on Edith's face back against the skull, sharpening the bones. Her hairline has retreated to reveal an expanse of pink scalp. Below, gravity has dropped the bulk of her body down into a large middle mass of belly and bottom, with skinny legs beneath.

Yes, a broody hen settled on her nest. Alert, slightly suspicious, equally ready to be attacked or entertained.

Jenna sighs, knowing she'll probably be exactly the same in twenty years.

She says, "Really, Edie? You don't remember? Mom told me over and over, not because it was funny but because she held a grudge against Dad for the rest of his life. It was your wedding day. In June, right? 1954? When you married Rob? The reception was at the farm, right? I was the flower girl. I was only three and I don't remember it. But Mom told me that Dad was supposed to clean out the big henhouse a week before the wedding. But he procrastinated. He left it until the day before and when he shoveled all the smelly chicken shit into the manure spreader, he filled it too full and the spreader leaked all over the driveway. It was June, it was hot, and Mom said the yard stank to high heaven. There was no time and no way to clean it up before the wedding guests arrived. Everyone did their best to ignore the smell, but Mom was furious. That's what she told me."

"No." Edith shakes her head hard. "No! I know nothing about that." She snaps, "And *do not use* that filthy language around me, young lady."

Jenna spreads chicken salad onto stale bread. She hides her smile from Edie. "Mom was so embarrassed. And so mad at Dad, she told me, she didn't talk to him for a week. Of all the times to clean the chicken coop, he had to do it right then? And your new mother-in-law, what was her name? Dorothy. She was very high-society, an old-money Mayflower descendant. A granddaughter of a Massachusetts governor, I think. She didn't approve of her son marrying the farmer's daughter anyway—"

"No! It did not happen that way!" Edith shouts. "Our wedding was perfect, Rob and I were so happy, it was a beautiful day in June! Everyone should have a June wedding! I was so pretty and it was perfect." Tears glaze her eyes.

"Yes," Jenna concedes, "you were very pretty. But every time Mom looked at your wedding picture, up there on the mantle over the fireplace, it reminded her of the smell, and she had to tell me that story. She said how unhappy she was with Dad that day. It wasn't about you, really. And," Jenna adds, "I'm sixty-eight. I can say 'shit' if I want to."

Edith twists her face away. "Why are you here? I don't want you here if you're going to tell lies and use filthy language."

"Because you need someone to help you. I'm your sister. I'm all the family you've got left."

Edith sets her mouth in a furious narrow line. In silence, Jenna serves their sandwiches and pours two glasses of milk.

With the food in front of her, Edith forgets to be angry. She shakes herself like a hen fluffing off dust. Smiling her sweet child's smile, she picks up her sandwich.

"That is the prettiest amaryllis, isn't it? I do love a spot of red in the room." Mouth full of chicken salad, Edie points a finger at the windowsill where a glass tumbler holds a stalk of bright green with four brilliant blooms rising from a bulb that Jenna had brought a few weeks earlier.

Jenna sighs and sits down, thinking: We share blood, but not much else.

They had never lived together. Never spent more than a few hours in each other's company until a year ago when Edith's husband died. Childless, Edith downsized into a studio apartment and offered Jenna a stipend to help clean and cook. Jenna—divorced, living alone, with her one grown son working abroad—figured it was an opportunity to strengthen family ties. Maybe learn some hidden truths about her little-known siblings and long-dead parents. And she needed the money.

What Jenna had gained in that year, along with several shifting versions of family stories, was the suspicion that her older sister had probably always skated on the thin edge of truth. Every visit with Edith included some sort of verbal barrage, a slew of distracting non sequiturs, casual criticisms, and unverifiable reminiscences. The random chatter and rapidly shifting moods, fueled by age and untethered impulses, created a cognitive whiplash that left Jenna feeling manipulated and exhausted. Could she comb through all that clutter to find a few small truths about herself, her family, or anything else? Probably not.

So now the topic is flowers, which Jenna figures is safe enough. Edith natters on through lunch, speaking of vases and past floral arrangements and how much she loves sunflowers. She falls silent, briefly, while Jenna gathers the plates and fills the sink with soapy dishwater. Then, despising a conversational vacuum, Edith launches into her favorite topic, the rhetorical tale of Our Perfect Childhood.

"We had the best parents ever, didn't we? And the best life on the farm. What a wonderful place to grow up, out there in God's green country. It was perfect, wasn't it?" She looks to Jenna for agreement. Jenna knows she's supposed to chime in, to say oh yes, absolutely, the best childhood, the best parents, we were so fortunate. Yes, it was God's country. Remember the wild blueberries we picked, the strawberries that Daddy planted, the corn that grew so tall, the kittens born in the haymow.

She isn't sure where Edie is going with it this time, but Jenna is tired of being spoken to as if she were a simple child or an echo chamber for Edie's fables. She just doesn't have the energy today to consume that much saccharine.

Jenna drains the sink. "Edie, maybe you remember that it was lovely and perfect, but I know you all had a hard life during the Depression. Our brothers fought in the Second World War. And Dad had a thing for Mom's younger sister."

Jenna is worn out and her own filters are starting to fail. But she can't stop now. "After he lost the farm, Dad spent the family savings on grand ideas that didn't work. Remember? He tried selling insurance but failed at that, too, and that's when Mom had to go to work as a lunch lady at the high school. Finally, Dad got a job as a school janitor. At least he had health insurance when he got cancer."

"I don't remember any of that."

"I guess you don't. That last part, after the farm got sold? That was during *my* childhood, not yours. I had a pretty good childhood, too, but it wasn't perfect. Nothing is perfect. And gods don't have countries, as far as I know, so I really don't get that part."

Edith looks away, her mouth set in a stubborn line.

As Jenna sponges crumbs off the table, Edith catches her wrist in one arthritic hand and grips fiercely.

"Jenna, you always were a contrary child. Our mother spoiled you rotten. That's why I moved out when you were two."

"Yeah, you've said that. A lot."

"Why are you always so disagreeable? Why can't you just agree with me? I don't *want* to remember anything bad or hurtful. I only want to talk about nice things. Pretty things!"

Jenna ignores the sharp fingernails digging into her skin and lets her wrist go limp. "I guess," she sighs, "what I want to hear is something *true*. Life isn't pretty, most of the time. We learn from the tough parts. The way you tell it, everything was always so perfect and sweet and lovely. But I know it wasn't."

Edith is silent for several seconds. She lets go of Jenna and folds her hands on the table in front of her. "Well, then," she says with a secretive smile. "You do know why Mom got pregnant, right?"

Whiplashed again. Damn, some days it's hard to keep up.

Jenna searches her memory for something to contribute, since Edith might now offer information on something more substantial than flowers.

"Well," Jenna begins, "Mom told me she got pregnant that first time when she was barely fifteen, with Martha, because she wanted to get away from caring for all her little sisters and brothers. If she was going to take care of babies, she said, they should be her own. She wanted to marry a farmer, Dad was a handsome young farmer, and I guess she figured that was a good way to catch him. At the time Dad had another girlfriend, Corinne, right? His family expected he'd marry Corinne, so Mom was pretty proud that he married her instead."

Jenna rattles on. "Then Mom had the next three kids, Allen and you and Charlie. She told me she didn't know anything about birth control, and of course it was illegal then. An aunt finally told her how to get a diaphragm. So no more babies for a long time. But two decades later, at age 41, she got pregnant one more time—surprise!—and there I was, after everyone else was grown and gone."

Jenna stacks the dried plates on a shelf over the sink and wonders briefly why they're discussing Mom's pregnancies.

Is this a lead-in to a discussion about sex? Does Edith want to know more about Jenna's wild party-girl life during the sixties, as part of "getting to know all about you?" Please, no.

"She got pregnant with you," Edith intones dramatically, "to save her marriage."

"Wait, what?"

"It was because of Daddy's old girlfriend, Corinne. He was married to Mother for twenty-five years, working on the farm and raising us four. But Daddy never forgot Corinne. He wrote to her all those years, and she wrote back. She got married and was living in Virginia. Then her husband died, maybe in '48 or '49. Dad told Mom he wanted a divorce so he could go marry Corinne. We were all grown up, see? Martha was married, Allen was in college. Charlie had good jobs and Charlie had a steady girl. Dad figured he'd done his duty and twenty-five years was enough."

Jenna chucks the dish towel onto the counter, returns to the table and sits with a thump. "Dad told her he wanted to leave? That's a hell of a mid-life crisis."

Edith frowns. "Don't say 'hell,'" she says automatically. "So what she did is, she got herself pregnant with you. Then Dad had to stay. To support you, right? You got born and that saved the family! Though I guess Corinne wouldn't have him anyway. She turned him down. Said she wouldn't be a homewrecker."

"How do you know all this? Who told you?"

"Mother did, about a year after you were born. So you see, Jenna," Edith says with an air of triumph, "I *do* know a few things about you. Things that you don't even know. You were Mom's miracle baby! What do you think about *that*?"

Jenna has no idea what to think. She begins slowly. "I think...it's pretty sad, actually. I guess I feel bad for Dad, living all those years with Mom but secretly wishing he'd married Corinne. He must have felt so manipulated. I'm sad for Mom, too, that she thought she had to use pregnancy to keep Dad tied down. I guess she felt she had no other options. It's a sad story all around, if it's true."

Edith's nostrils flare. She sucks in a sharp breath.

"What do you mean *if it's true?*" she shouts. "And you're missing the point! It's not a story, it's the truth. It's not sad, it's wonderful. Mom was so clever! She found a way to keep the family together. Babies are supposed to be wanted and you were *wanted*. It was a miracle, God caused you to be born to save the family. That's why we all were so happy when you were born, why we all loved you."

Jenna gazes at the stranger in the wheelchair, this angry old woman that everyone says is her sister. What can she say? If you loved me, you'd have been there when I ran away from home because I felt lost and alone after Dad died. You missed my high school and college graduations. You never met my first fiancé. You missed all three of my weddings, one abortion, two divorces, my son's birth, and all the rest of the first sixty-five years of my life. Please, tell me *how* you've loved me.

"Let's leave gods and miracles out of it," Jenna finally says. "If that's the way it happened, it was Mom's plan, not anyone else's. But you're saying I accomplished this grand purpose in life just by getting born? And that's why my family loved me?" She pauses, thinking. "If Corinne turned him down, was I even necessary?"

"I don't know that! And it doesn't matter! The point is, we loved you." The words come automatically but Edie says it like she's trying to convince herself. "And Mother was happy, and Dad stayed, so it worked and the rest of us didn't have to worry about them getting divorced. Like I said, that's what mattered most."

They stare at each other over the impasse. Then Edie's shoulders sag. "You must have been lonely."

Sighing, Jenna slumps back in her chair. "Dad must have found some way," she says slowly, "to make peace with Mom because yes, I had a good childhood. I'm sure you four older ones were jealous. Yes, I was spoiled. But you're wrong, I was never lonely. I preferred to be alone. I still do."

She hesitates. "Edie, I'm sorry. There's really no way to catch up properly, is there?"

Edith's eyes fill with tears. "Of course you were spoiled. You were the special one. And we *are* catching up."

She wipes a trembling hand over her eyes and sighs. "You're right. About my wedding reception. The reason Mother was so angry with Daddy? My new mother-in-law, Dorothy, that high-society lady as you call her—she stepped in it. In the chicken shit. Yes, Mother spoke of that every time she looked at my wedding pictures. Daddy spread it but Mother kept talking about it. They ruined that day for me, both of them. I do remember, of course I do. But I choose not to."

Jenna's voice softens. "I know, Edie. But you kept your head up, you kept going. Sometimes that's all we can do.

"And Edie? It's book, lamp, table." She places an arm awkwardly around her sister's thin, bony shoulders and gives her a small hug. "Next time, you'll remember."

FISHING

Three of Jake's buddies flew directly from Afghanistan into intensive rehab for amputees. Another came home in a body bag. Jake got dropped off back home with a medal, a large bottle of anti-depressants, and a referral to a therapist.

A week after he emptied his duffle bag and peeled the Metallica posters off the wall of his old room, he still wasn't talking much. Not knowing what to do, his kid sister SueEllen proposed a walk down by the creek or around the used-to-be soybean fields out behind their double-wide. She thought that might ease his mind, seeing the old places they'd played as kids. But the fields were fallow, gone to weeds and briars. Surveyors had strung pink tape like party flags on sweetgums by the creek, reminding them that it wasn't granddaddy's land anymore. The developer was just waiting on subdivision approval.

Jake said he didn't want to see any of that. When SueEllen suggested a fishing trip instead, he agreed that might be okay. They could go to the flooded quarry where they used to trawl for brim and those ugly catfish. Their momma always complained about all the bones, but brim and catfish were both pretty good if you skinned them first, then dredged them in cornmeal and fried them up with okra and tomatoes.

SueEllen arranged a day off from the diner and asked their cousin Marvin about borrowing his rowboat and two fishing poles. She found hooks, bobbers, and sinkers in the old tool shed, and gave Jake the pole with the working reel.

"And worms. I got us these night-crawlers," she sad as they hauled the dinged-up aluminum rowboat out of Marvin's pickup at the quarry. She showed Jake the Duke's mayonnaise jar filled with dirt. "Norwood had them at the store, two dollar a dozen."

Jake pushed the boat off the rocks and rowed them to the middle of the quarry lake, the oars slapping hard on the black water. But when he went to thread a worm onto his hook, his fingers trembled too hard. He sat in silence while SueEllen baited her own hook and hung a pole over the stern.

"I think it'd be better," she said, "if it was springtime. Summer's too hot, we've had this drought for weeks. Sorry you had to come home to this."

She waited for him to say something, but he just folded one hand over the other to quiet the trembling and stared at the harsh sunlight glinting off the surface of the gouged-out lake. There was no breeze and no sound, no bird calls or even insects humming over the water.

They'd rowed out too deep for catfish and nothing else was biting.

After an hour in the sun, the soil in the mayonnaise jar had dried out. Not seeing any point to keeping the worms, SueEllen moved to empty the jar over the gunwale. She figured they could feed the fish they weren't catching, maybe make them fatter for next time.

"No," Jake said. "Let's take them home. Put them where the garden used to be. You dump them here, they'll just drown."

SueEllen frowned down into the half-sideways Duke's jar. "They're just worms."

He stared at the water. "Nothing is 'just' anything."

"What?"

"First, there's too much sound. All the screaming. But when there's no sound, it's worse. First you hear the scream and then you hear the silence."

"They're just worms," she said again, confused. "Worms don't make sounds. Might as well give the fish a treat."

"That's the worst part, see? When something's dying, and it doesn't make a sound."

Jake took the jar from her and splashed a handful of lake water onto the parched soil. He cradled it in his lap and closed his eyes against the sun. She picked up the oars and rowed them back to shore.

THE CAT

When I get home from work, our housemate Travis sits fidgeting on the porch steps, rotating an empty beer bottle and picking at the label.

"I'm clearing out," he tells me. He stands, sets the bottle on the porch railing, and stares into the woods. "He shot your cat."

Maybe I heard it wrong. "What cat?"

Stupid question. There is only one cat. My cat, Misha, a creamy seal-point Siamese with green eyes and a crooked tail. He appeared on the doorstep one evening a month ago, right after the neighbors moved away. Misha lives with me, my husband, my husband's buddy Travis, and a mongrel hound they found in the woods. The mutt chases the cat and barks at everyone and digs holes in the yard. The cat scratches and hisses and steals the dog's food.

Travis looks down and digs a toe into the rotten spot on the porch floor. "Your cat. Your husband shot him."

I lean my bike against the pin-oak tree, the big one that's hanging two dead limbs over the roof of our house trailer. The next storm will probably take out the front bedroom or maybe the whole single-wide. Then we'll have to move, not necessarily a bad thing.

Next to Travis's feet is a half-collapsed cardboard box that holds all his possessions. It's exactly the size and same saggy shape of the passenger seat in his beat-up Miata. There's never been room in that car for anything else, just Travis, his ratty old box of socks and underwear, and a constantly shifting pile of books, mostly math and physics, on the car's floor. He doesn't have to say he's leaving, I see the box.

"Your cat," he repeats. "Misha." This sounds like an apology but I'm pretty sure it's not his fault.

I'm tired and sweaty and my shirt stinks of mint chocolate chip. Friday's special, two scoops in a waffle cone, half-price. The middle schoolers swarmed for that one. We ran out and I had to grab two new tubs from the supercold freezer. My right arm aches from chopping chunks of rock-hard ice cream that never softened enough to be scoopable. It's still summer but I'm cold and aching everywhere.

I say, "When?" Like that matters.

"Noon-ish. He went outdoors and I heard him yelling about something. He ran in, grabbed the rifle, ran out. I heard three shots. I asked him what the hell, dude, but he just threw the gun down and said he was gonna be late for work. Then he left."

"You've been waiting for me since noon?"

Travis nods. Picks up his box and fumbles it a little because it's threatening to break open at the seams. Or maybe his hands are shaking.

"I can't—" He takes a breath, starts over. "Rent's paid to the end of the month. We're square."

"Please don't go." Finally I've found something I want to say but it's too late.

He clears his throat. "Julie, you loved that damned cat. It cried all the time and it was always fighting with the dog. That was a terrible cat. But you loved it."

"Yes." Not sure what I was agreeing to, the love or the terribleness or both.

"But he hated it. Hell, I hated it too. But it was your cat and you loved it."

"*Three* shots? No, never mind. Where is he?"

He knows I'm not asking about my husband. "I buried him under the raspberries." He points to where a dozen thorny, skin-ripping canes curve over the grass at the edge of the woods. Now I smell it, that rich garden scent of fresh-turned earth.

Travis still isn't looking at me. "I'll wait while you pack. Give you a ride to wherever. I'll make room in the Miata. You can hold the box on your lap."

As far as I know, Travis has never offered anyone a ride in his car.

"It's okay," I tell him. "But thanks anyway."

He and the box pivot to face me. "Seriously?" His eyes are mossy green, unreadable. Same as always.

"I'll stay," I tell him. "I'll deal with it."

His shoulders sag. Whatever we were—battle buddies, comrades, the three amigos—it's over. He turns away, heads for his car.

I need a shower. Then I'll put on my yellow sundress and feed the stupid dog and make dinner. Pick some string beans, assemble a meat loaf.

When the one I married gets home at seven-fifteen, I'll be waiting on the porch steps with the rifle across my lap. I'll tell him that Travis, his best friend from way back plus four tours in Afghanistan, has moved out. And no, I didn't ask where.

Once I have his attention, I'll explain that I've hidden the ammunition. If he's still listening, I'll talk about my day. All the things I did and didn't do. How I grabbed his favorite guitar by its neck and took a couple of practice swings, planning to smash it, but changed my mind and set it back in its proper place on the shelf beside our bed. I'll tell him about the dinner I made, meat loaf and beans, and how I wanted to fling it into the gulley but instead it's waiting now in the oven. And maybe in a little while we can eat together, just the two of us.

And then I'll ask him to please explain why he shot my cat.

Maybe he'll tell me, maybe he won't.

Reading the Cards

At five-fifty AM the stench of day-old fryer grease tangles with the odors of burnt coffee and the lard-heavy biscuits cooling on the baker's rack. When the smell hits, Cassie's gut lurches a little. She steadies herself against the doorframe and takes a few deep breaths before plucking a fresh apron off the diner's supply shelf.

The queasiness subsides but a memory surfaces and suddenly she's back in a hospital waiting room, she can't remember which one. It always smelled like this at mealtimes, when orderlies hustled food carts down the corridors and anxious parents fidgeted with cardboard cups of cold coffee.

Start with the aroma of her parents' diner, then blend in the scent of urine and that peculiar metallic odor of blood. Add some disinfectant and a dirty diaper or a touch of vomit and there you are, right back in the pediatrics wing.

Two blinks and a shiver, and Cassie's returned to the kitchen. Her husband Luke sits hunched over a textbook in their breakroom spot, a cheap plastic table set with two plastic chairs set next to the baker's rack.

"Time to get cooking, hon." She drapes a black cook's apron over the shoulder of his black tee shirt and touches a gentle finger to his dark chin stubble. He shifts his gaze to her face and frowns slightly. For a moment she thinks he might be struggling to recognize her.

She hopes it's just eyestrain because he's only twenty-three and they absolutely don't have money for an eye doctor. He reads so much that his eyes often look glazed-over, faded like a dried-out lawn that once was green but now is brown. Dry and worn down and too quiet, just waiting for winter.

Cassie needs him here in the present so she gently bumps his shoulder with a hip. He yawns and flicks his left thumbnail against his index finger a couple of times, like brushing off dirt. It's how he pulls himself out of a mind-drift. His hands are rough and chapped from all the dishwashing, but the pad of his index finger where the thumbnail strikes is worn raw.

He stretches, rolls his shoulders, and tucks a paper napkin into chapter seven of John Merriman's *A History of Modern Europe, Volume Two*, liberally marked with yellow highlighter.

The diner's front door creaks and there's a swirl of voices as the first customers push in. Cassie peers through the gap in the kitchen's swinging doors as people pull off face masks, claim stools at the chrome-edged counter, and slide into red-vinyl booth seats by the front windows. The overhead fans rotate lazily, barely stirring the humid September air.

Luke is on his feet now so Cassie walks through to the front with her order pad out and her smile in place. She pulls on gloves and secures a face mask, moves a full coffee pot to the back burner, and starts the decaf. Lines up mugs and pours the fire chief's coffee right away before he sits down because he's always in a rush.

This crowd doesn't need menus. The specials haven't changed in years. She listens, nods, confirms orders. Keeps the smile in place because customers expect it and that's how you earn tips.

At the grill, head cook Marcus is cracking eggs and flattening strips of fatty bacon. Slapping out sausage patties, pouring out pancake batter. A former Army mess cook with rude tattoos and no patience for slackers, he wields his forks and spatulas with an angry energy.

"Where you been, man?" he calls over a shoulder. Dark eyes squint against the grill heat. "We got hungry people here. Oil's hot so drop those taters in, fry boy. Get them sizzlin. An' we need toast to be toastin. Make that white bread go all crispy brown."

"And get your damn mask on," Marcus adds, "at least where people can see you. You get us shut down again, I'm puttin you *in* the fry-o-lator."

Luke wraps apron strings around his narrow waist and creates an awkward knot that he'll have to re-tie twice by six-thirty. He fumbles a blue paper face mask into place and shakes out frozen chunks of potato. The hot oil roils and spits as he drops wire baskets into the fryer wells.

From the front of the pass shelf Cassie and Raven, their other server, slide their scribbled order slips over to Marcus. Eggs and toast, white because it's all they offer. Pancakes with cheap syrup. Fat-laden local sausage and burnt-crisp bacon. Biscuits and grits and home fries. Store-bought pies, blackberry and pecan and achingly sweet chess pie.

The Shotswell Diner Gas & Groc. has existed in Dry Ridge forever, like Cassie's family and Cassie herself. At age six, she was laying out silverware and napkins. At twelve, she cleaned restrooms and kept the coffee brewing. She graduated to waitressing at fifteen, burger-flipping at sixteen. Now at twenty-two, it's all that plus paying the vendors and balancing the accounts. Schoolwork, social activities, and occasional nights out have always been sandwiched in between all those hours at the diner.

At full capacity, the diner seats twenty-eight people plus take-out. It opens at six and closes at three, six days a week. Friday is payday. On Sundays, Cassie drives her parents to New Bethlehem Baptist, then sits in the church parking lot reading a romance or juggling their paper-thin finances while Luke goes to the laundromat to bleach out grease and ketchup stains from their work clothes. Evenings, he reads and re-reads his textbooks while Cassie watches whatever the TV antenna can pick up.

Once—it seems long ago but it was only three years— they had friends and a social life. That was in high school and the first few months into Luke's freshman year at NC State. Now their friends have drifted or faded or run away.

And this COVID thing has settled in. Not the first virus they've dealt with, but still a scary one, and anyway there's no time or money for nights out. So far they've dodged the virus and Cassie tries to feel grateful. She and Luke get regular meals, regular paychecks, and bare-bones medical insurance. Lots of people have it way worse, probably.

With the long hours and hard work and all the extra cleaning needed on account of the virus, Cassie seldom gets to eat lunch at the same time as her husband but sometimes she and Raven can grab a burger together and share a table after the lunch crowd clears out.

Today, a Tuesday, the diner's quiet by two-thirty. Marcus is gone and Luke's out back in the steamy kitchen, scrubbing pans and shoving the last rack of dirty plates through the dishwasher. At the sandwich board, Cassie assembles a BLT and pours a glass of milk. She slides into a vinyl-seated booth across from Raven, who's got her usual cheeseburger and Pepsi.

Raven, birthname Regina, has been working at the diner for six weeks, ever since the corona virus restrictions eased and the diner went back to full capacity. At the start of the pandemic, Cassie's parents moved across the parking lot to manage the grocery part of the store, leaving Cassie, Marcus and Luke to keep the diner going with phone orders, take-out, and local delivery. The recent return of their eat-in customers had prompted the hiring of a second server.

Raven tells people she's half Cherokee and all country. She wears pearl-snap cowgirl shirts and lots of turquoise and dyes her long brown hair jet black because she says that's what people expect an Indian to have. She also insists she's inherited psychic skills from her mother's clan and the diner job is just temporary until she gets good enough to go professional. She's memorized The Eight Must-Have Skills of Tarot Readers, and she's got a brand-new website that offers private psychic readings on Zoom.

So far Cassie's managed to avoid having her cards read or her fortunes revealed by Raven. But now she sees, too late, that there's a set of Tarot cards stacked face-down near the saltshaker.

Raven pushes aside her half-eaten burger and grins. "Hey girl, good news! I was waitin to tell you, I got my Zoom set up. But I need more practice, so I'll do yours for free, okay?"

Mouth full of BLT, Cassie shakes her head. Raven isn't discouraged. She picks up the cards and begins an awkward sorting routine. The cards are stiff, obviously new.

Raven clears her throat. "I'm shuffling these cards to get rid of the energy from the last reading. While I'm doing this, you're supposed to think about what parts of your life need clarity. And what questions you want to ask the cards."

Cassie sighs. She nudges her plate and glass closer to the wall, to avoid interfering with whatever Raven or the cards might do in the center of the table. "I don't need clarity, just food. Let me eat, huh?"

"Well yeah, that's okay. You can keep eatin, I won't stop you. You should be hungry, you don't eat enough anyway for a kitten. Let's find you some inner strength, okay? It's all in the cards, the cards don't lie." Raven taps the stack. "So, first you need to choose three from here."

Cassie points to her mouth, still chewing, so Raven turns over the top cards. "The three-card spread, see, this tells us about the question you're asking."

Cassie swallows. "I'm not asking a question. I'm eating a sandwich."

Raven persists. "This is where you can absorb your emotions. Reflect on the symbols."

"I can't *reflect* on the symbols if I can't *see* the symbols. And I don't know what the symbols mean. And I don't believe any of it anyway. I'm supposed to 'absorb my emotions?' What the hell does that mean?" Cassie wants to leave but she also wants to finish eating. And she's afraid of offending Raven who is a good worker.

If she eats faster, maybe she can get away sooner.

Raven leans forward and tries to catch Cassie's eye. Cassie ignores her. Chews, swallows. Pushes a stray piece of lettuce into her mouth, not caring if it sticks to her teeth.

Raven flips over several new cards. "Look!"

Defeated, Cassie abandons the last bite of sandwich. She wipes her hands on a paper napkin and finger-combs her short brown hair. She's probably just smeared bacon grease or mayonnaise into her curls, but she doesn't care.

Cassie sighs. "Okay, what?"

Delighted, Raven smiles and taps two cards with orange-lacquered fingernails. She slides them toward Cassie. "Well lookee here. It's the Lovers, next to the Empress! Love and creativity! There's going to be—" She pauses and spreads her hands palms up for dramatic effect. "A baby! There's a baby wanting to get born. Wanting to come to you!" She waves the cards. "Wow, I've never turned up that combination before!"

Cassie stiffens. She leans back, bracing her hands against the plastic tabletop. "A baby? No way. You're crazy, or your cards are crazy. Believe me, I'd know if I was pregnant." Her eyes fill and she slides out of the booth, getting ready to stand.

Raven is performing now. Her voice goes sing-songy. "The cards say you are ready to embrace hope again, to renew that great motherhood adventure. So, are you on that path?" She raises an eyebrow and flashes a share-it-with-me smile.

"No. *No.*" Cassie's breath catches. She pauses at the edge of the cracked vinyl seat.

"Seriously, Cass." Raven drops the spiel and leans in. "Have you peed on the stick yet? You're wearin that look.

Dark around the eyes but kind of glowin, too. Yeah, there's definitely something hormone-y going on. But," she adds in a big-sister voice, "you are *way* too skinny. Gotta get some weight on those bones, girl."

"*No.*" Cassie groans, thinking, *Dammit, Raven means well but she doesn't have a clue.* "Look, I think I'd know. And it's not possible anyway. I'm on the patch, not the path. Whatever that is… So no, no way."

Raven reaches a hand over the table but Cassie twists aside, looking at the wall clock over the grill. Almost three. Time to lock up, cash out, clean up. She stands and sweeps sandwich crumbs off her black jeans.

Her co-worker's voice goes syrupy with sympathy. "It must be a terrible thing, Cass. Losing the baby like you did. I know it was terrible for you, Luke too, but you can't give up. You can try again."

"Who told you?" Cassie snaps.

Raven pulls back, offended. "Marcus."

"You don't know anything about it and it's totally none of your business. I absolutely *cannot* get pregnant."

Raven scoops up her cards and slides out of the booth. "Oh, I'm sure you can." Her voice tips from annoyed to assured. "You had one baby, of course you can have another. It was SIDS, right? That sudden-death thing. Doctors can't explain that, it just happens. There was nothing you could've done."

Cassie is sick of people telling her what she should do. "You really *don't* understand. It's a *must not* thing, not a *cannot* thing. Her name was Sophie and it wasn't SIDS. There were—complications. She was born defective."

"That's a horrible thing to say, calling a baby defective. Every baby deserves love." She steps closer, dangly turquoise earrings trembling. "Maybe God had plans you just don't know about, so he touched your little girl in a special way. Then he called her home early."

Damn, Cassie thinks. *I've heard that so freaking many times.*

"That's what the bible tells us," Raven adds firmly. "And that's from the Tarot cards, too, you know, finding meaning in all those random things that just seem to happen. It all *means* something."

Cassie's throat catches. She spins away and nearly collides with Luke. He steps aside, wiping chapped red hands on a wrinkled towel as Cassie pushes past, heading for the kitchen.

For a moment his eyes follow Cassie but then he scowls at Raven instead. "No. The baby was defective. If something's born with defects, then it's defective."

Raven flushes pink. She turns the other way and barges out the diner's front door, black hair swirling. Luke follows her to the door, flips the deadbolt lock, and turns the window sign from OPEN to CLOSED. He stoops over the booth where Raven and Cassie had been sitting and wipes the table clean in large, slow circles.

Behind the diner, Cassie stumbles across the weedy backyard, breathing hard, and stops to lean against the wooden shed that houses the diner's trash bins and the fry-grease tank.

She sinks to the ground. Sits, wraps her arms around her knees, and collapses sideways against the shed's rough boards. Closes hot wet eyes against the brightness of the late-summer day and waits for her heart to stop pounding.

Dammit, she wants a cigarette. But three years ago, when she was nineteen and newly pregnant, she'd promised herself—and Luke, and her unborn baby—that she'd never smoke again. She just needs a minute to get herself together so she can go back inside to finish up.

This evening, when she stops at CVS to pick up Luke's meds, she'll get a pregnancy kit too. Just to be sure.

***

Four years earlier, high school sweethearts Cassie (voted Most Popular, Cutest) and Luke (Brainiest, Most Likely to Succeed) believed they'd mapped out their perfect future. The day after graduation and two weeks before their wedding, they wrote it all down on a heart-shaped, lace-trimmed card and gave it a title: "Lucas and Cassandra—Our Life Together."

Cassie used her pretty schoolgirl cursive, so rarely taught anymore, to write out their goals: Work, School, Family. Luke added some optimistic budget figures. They signed their names with flourishes and posted the heart card on the refrigerator in the single-wide trailer they'd rented from her parents.

Cassie's parents were cautiously pleased. They agreed Luke was a catch, she was marrying up. But privately? "You're both too young," her mother said. "Wait a few years."

Luke's father and mother were clearly dismayed. They'd wanted him to get his degree and start teaching before getting tied down in marriage. Three months after the wedding, his parents and Luke's younger brother Ethan moved from western North Carolina to Miami. His father said he'd been offered a new position in his insurance company, but Cassie suspected they wanted to put some distance between themselves and their new in-laws, her dad the gas station manager and her mom the grocery clerk.

Cassie and Luke assured each other their parents would come around after a year or two, after they saw how well The Plan was working. According to Our Life Together, Cassie would stay employed full-time at her parents' diner while Luke earned his teaching degree at NC State. There was a teacher shortage, so Luke knew he'd land a good job right after graduation. He was passionate about teaching high school history.

Then Cassie would go for a two-year certificate from the community college. She'd be in healthcare, nursing or dental assistant or lab tech. She was a little vague about exactly what, but she was pretty sure that, after six years of living frugally and saving their pennies, they'd be on track to buy a small house. Something older, a starter home in a good neighborhood. Then children. Two, maybe three.

Except this happened: Eight months after adding the hearts and lace to Our Life Together, right after freshman-year spring break at Luke's parents' place in Miami, Cassie learned she was pregnant.

Well, okay, Luke said. The first baby is a few years ahead of schedule. Our parents will help. We'll manage.

"If it's a boy," Cassie said, "we'll name him Ryan, after my grandfather."

"If it's a girl," Luke said, "We'll name her Sophie, for my grandmother. Sophie means 'wisdom and light.'"

The baby, a premature girl born blue-skinned and weak on a gray November morning, arrived with a full head of dark hair but was missing one-third of her brain. Microcephaly, the obstetrician said sadly. She'll have trouble swallowing. There's nerve damage. She has a hearing problem and her eyes don't track properly. She may live a few months, maybe longer.

A few days after the birth, when the overwhelming shock had subsided to a pervasive general despair, Luke and Cassie named her Sophie anyway. "We need to stay positive," Cassie told Luke before she understood what lay ahead.

"Pray," Cassie's mother urged them. "You're not praying hard enough."

"Luke has to drop out of school," her father told them. "Get a full-time job. He can work at the diner if he can't find anything else. We'll cover the rent and help with food, that's the best we can do."

Luke's parents sent them a Christmas card with a check for five thousand dollars. They never spoke of their first granddaughter.

The doctors had plenty to say, endlessly interrogating Cassie and Luke about their health histories and sex life. What about measles, strep, flu, HIV, syphilis, meningitis? Did you use condoms, birth control pills, antidepressants? Smoke, drink? Use heroin or cocaine or meth or marijuana?

And what about travel? Have you heard of Zika virus? When you were in Miami, were either of you bitten by a mosquito? Did you have any flu-like symptoms? Zika can be transferred from person to person during sex, did you know that? Did you know the fetus can be infected through the mother?

Cassie remembered having a headache and a rash, two days after snorkeling on Key Largo.

If it was Zika, the doctors couldn't confirm it. She should have gotten tested earlier, they said. Earlier tests might have revealed something.

That was when Luke blew up in the pediatrician's office, yelling and hurling furniture until security was called.

"So," he screamed, "we're *fucking guilty*? Guilty of going to Miami to see my parents, guilty of having sex while married? Guilty of not getting tested earlier for a virus we didn't even fucking *know about*?"

Anti-depressants were prescribed for Cassie, mood balancers for Luke. And many, many drugs for Sophie to control epilepsy, improve breathing, and ease the near-paralysis in her limbs.

Cassie and Luke spent their days in terror and chaos. Your baby will need round-the-clock care, the patient liaison said. You'll need to learn about Medicaid. What's covered, how to file, where to get nursing services and durable medical equipment. Here's instructions for feeding, a list of what she needs each day. Sensory exercises and home-based PT. Later, she'll need botox injections to relax her stiffened limbs, glasses for vision correction. Hearing aids and cochlear implants.

Cassie's determination to remain optimistic dissolved in fury and shame and a fierce urge to dig her nails into the face of every doctor who peered at their daughter in pity or fascination.

Luke went the other way, falling into numb silences and a deep despair. He showed little interest in his daughter and touched her only when necessary. He disappeared into his textbooks, dropped weight, and sagged under the pain of their daughter's burdens as they sat in endless waiting rooms and moved slowly through the halls of hospitals, and doctors' offices, and the infants' ICU.

When Sophie was eight weeks old they brought her home to their two-bedroom mobile home. She was accompanied by a day nurse, a truckload of medical equipment, and a list of upcoming appointments.

"It *has* to get better," Cassie told Luke. They'd figure out how to live with this, and they'd find a way to pay off the crushing medical bills. Go on food stamps and welfare. Declare bankruptcy.

At nine months, Sophie began having seizures. Her new pediatrician explained that the nerves misfire, causing oxygen deprivation. Sophie needed extra oxygen, delivered through a nasal cannula while she was awake and a face mask while she slept. The mask had to be strapped over her face each evening and checked every two hours because she sometimes cried and thrashed and knocked it off. They got a baby monitor and set the volume on high.

The doctors were encouraged by Sophie's progress, so they updated the prognosis. She might live for four or five years, maybe longer, if no other complications surfaced.

A week after the oxygen compressor took up residence next to Sophie's crib in the cramped second bedroom, the beautiful lace-trimmed card proclaiming Our Life Together vanished from the refrigerator. Neither mentioned it.

They learned how much good nursing care costs and how little they could afford it. So they juggled schedules and budgets and took care of their daughter themselves. They moved through their days in great chunks of silence, Luke tending to fryolators and dishwashers, Cassie tending to Sophie's never-ending care. At night they took turns checking her breathing mask. Every two hours, faithfully following the doctors' orders.

Cassie and Luke found their only comfort in each other's bodies. When both were still awake after checking Sophie's oxygen or changing her diaper, they met in exhausted, grim couplings that left their skin slick with sweat and their faces swollen with hot tears.

Sophie lived for almost two years. During that time, Cassie's parents gave them free rent, the use of an old car, a weekly box of day-old produce from the grocery, and two meals every day from the diner.

Her mother added a heavy dose of prayer and the not-so-veiled suggestion that Cassie and Luke must have done something sinful to bring such a terrible burden onto themselves and their families.

Her father stayed mostly silent and mainly invisible, working the gas pumps and stocking the shelves at the store. Tending to business so they'd all have a roof over their heads.

Friends from high school and college called once or twice, then disappeared. There were no invitations to a night out—what was the point?—and little reprieve from the never-ending care that Sophie required.

"You'd think my mother's minister would show up, at least," Cassie told Luke on Sophie's first birthday. "All those church dinners she's organized. Maybe this is supposed to push us back to the church. Or everyone's afraid our bad luck will rub off on them."

"It's the ultimate 'fuck off,'" Luke said. "We screwed up somehow. Messed up our perfect plan. They're wondering, what did we do to deserve this? Must've been something really bad, right?"

They did everything the doctors said to do, but in her two years of life Sophie never met a single milestone listed in the discarded baby books.

One morning, a week before Sophie's second birthday, Cassie rose at dawn in a quiet house to find the oxygen mask hissing softly beside Sophie's cooling body.

Luke had left for work an hour earlier and Cassie was alone with their daughter. Kneeling beside the crib, she cupped a hand around the small misshapen head.

Time stopped for however long it took her to remember that she needed to call 911. Then she gently tucked the yellow baby blanket around Sophie's already-cold body and waited for the paramedics to arrive.

Weeping, finally, and wondering when time would begin again.

***

Now, several hours after fleeing from Raven, Cassie's alone again in their trailer. She sits on the toilet and opens a test kit. Reads the instructions on the card and holds the stick with a shaking hand. Pees, then waits. Two lines appear, one dark and one a little lighter.

The second kit, a different brand, tells her the same thing.

How can this be? She's been careful, never late with a new patch. But she knows the odds. Slight, but not impossible.

The memories rush back and she knows how it will be. The exhaustion, the strange longings, the simultaneous hunger and nausea. The weight gain, the heavy breasts. Backaches, euphoria, random crying jags and, eventually, a feeling of power and strength and purpose.

But this time, everything will be painted with fear. She possesses a different wisdom now, a constant whisper that reminds her she can vow to do everything perfectly and still have everything go horribly wrong.

She wanders into the kitchen, opens the fridge, and stares. Closes it, not knowing what she's looking for. It's eight-thirty and dark outside. Her husband will be home soon, back from the coffeeshop where he uses the free wi-fi to upload his homework for his single online class.

The door swings open. Luke slides off his backpack and pours a glass of water. They sit on their fake-leather loveseat and Luke finds a college football game on TV. Neither cares about football, but this is what's on.

Cassie picks up the remote and mutes the game, readying herself.

Luke is doing that thing with his fingers again, flicking a thumbnail.

They both speak at once.

He says, "My dad called." Cassie blurts, "I'm pregnant."

Not how she'd planned to say it.

They stare at each other. Her gray eyes are wide and his hazel eyes are half-hidden by a shock of coffee-colored hair, uneven where she'd trimmed it for him. He didn't shave today, maybe not yesterday either. It's endearing, the stubble.

Distracted, she reaches up to touch his chin. Did he even hear what she said?

He frowns and pulls back a little. Starts again. "My dad called. He's got a friend who can give me a job in some tech company's research library, something to do with organizing their archives. Nearly full-time, with benefits, flexible hours so I can go to school, too. You can—you could get a restaurant job anywhere, right? Dad will help with the rent, too."

He breaks off, staring at her. "But you said—what?"

"I'm pregnant. I took the test, twice." She fights tears. "I can't believe it. We've been so careful! You *know* I've been careful. But—Miami? Really? I hate Miami. *You* hate Miami, you hated it even before—"

He takes her hands in his rough ones. "It's a second chance. A chance to get our life back on track."

That's exactly the phrase his father would use.

"But Miami? That's where I got the Zika virus!" She knows she's yelling, but she can't stop. "Now it's COVID, this stupid variant thing. It just goes on and on. And I'm *pregnant.*"

"Then maybe you need to be—not pregnant." He drops her hands and looks at the screen, where many small people in orange and blue uniforms are running in slow motion across impossibly green grass.

She grabs the remote again, switches off the TV. "Pregnancy is not a me thing, it's a we thing. You're saying that *we* need to be not pregnant."

"I—we—can't do this again." He turns to face her, imploring. "We can't be parents right now, not good ones."

"Not now? Or not ever?"

"Not—yet. I know it's a small risk, that the same thing would happen again, but—please, not yet. *Please.*"

She doesn't know which *same thing* he's talking about. Their daughter's birth, or their daughter's death?

She sags into his shoulder. "I get it. And part of me agrees. Yes, we need to—terminate." A pause. "I'm just so afraid. Of everything."

He slips an arm around her waist and draws her in.

"And I have to tell you something else." Her words are muffled against his gray sweatshirt. "About Sophie, the day she died." She pulls in a breath. "I overslept that morning. When I found her in her crib, I just stood there staring at her. I don't know how long, but—when her skin was cold, when I knew she was really truly gone, that's when I called 911." She pulls back to look up at him. "I took my time," she says. "At least I think I did. I don't remember it clearly. But do you understand?"

He nods.

She burrows into his chest again and lets the tears come. She feels the sharp, hard points of him—his shoulder, ribs, elbow, hip. We're both spread so thin, she thinks. Thinned and flattened like cardboard boxes left by the road. Crushed, just waiting to be recycled.

He brushes a curl gently back from her neck and runs a finger across her collarbone. He can't see her face so he looks at the small window next to the television where he can see a reflection of their blurred faces with only darkness behind.

"Maybe," he muses, "the strap on her mask wasn't as tight as it should've been. Maybe I should've checked it again before I left."

"I should've gotten up earlier—"

"You were worn out. Exhausted."

He waits until her tears are no more than hiccups, then he pulls her to her feet and leads her into their bedroom. He helps her undress.

"You were exhausted," he repeats, "so I turned down the volume on the monitor, see? To let you sleep."

PLAYING CHESS WITH BULLS

Two months ago, on Darcy's nineteenth birthday, I asked her why she rode bulls.

Part of it I get—the grit-and-rhinestone glamor of rodeos, the macho kick-ass allure of the cowboy culture.

But what flirty death wish compelled my sister to take up a sport like bull-riding? And how is it a *sport* to climb onto a pissed-off, three-quarter-ton beast—with horns—that wants to stomp you into the dirt?

Those china-blue eyes gleamed whenever she talked about the bulls. "It's like an eight-second game of chess. You have to out-think the moves your opponent's gonna make. The bull," she added, like I couldn't figure it out. "That's your opponent."

"Right," I said. "Chess."

She didn't hear my sarcasm and she was just spouting bullshit—*real* bullshit, right?—from the rodeo producer's PR campaign, their latest attempt at lipsticking a brutal gladiator event.

Darcy was all earnest, pleading for me to understand. "Bullriders are real religious, you know. There's a prayer we all say while we're gettin' our glove all rosined up. 'Lord ride with me.' Then you climb into the chute and ease down onto Mister Bull and just keep sayin' it, 'Lord ride with me Lord ride with me Lord ride with me.' Set your spurs and lean in. Finish it with 'By your grace I am saved.' Then everything explodes and it's awesome, the best adrenalin rush *ever*. Like a religious thing. Like ecstasy. Not the drug, the real thing."

"You joined a church?"

"No, it's just what we say."

"So riding bulls is like taking drugs?"

"*Way* better. Come watch me ride, Bets. Support your kid sister."

"I can't watch you do that. So, no."

But I do support her. I've been feeding her and her horse for the past two years. And after each smash-up with a bull—first a cracked collarbone and busted ribs, then a wired-up jaw and ruptured spleen—I convinced my husband Ryan to move his weights from the guest room to the garage so she could recuperate.

After a brindle Brahma named Bruisemaker broke her leg last spring, she stayed with me for three weeks. At the end of week one, Ryan let me know what he thought about that by slamming the back door off its hinges. He moved in with his cousin in Marshall and stayed there until I helped Darcy get good on crutches. I set her up in a Motel 6, the only place I could afford.

***

No one's heard from Darcy now for three days.

They found her truck at the post office yesterday, Monday morning. A mail carrier arriving early for work saw Darcy's rusted-out F-150, looking abandoned at the far side of the parking lot. The doors were unlocked and a key sat in plain sight on the dash. The left rear tire was flat. No spare.

The truck wouldn't start, a sheriff's deputy informed me over the phone. "The mailman recognized it. Told us you're her sister."

I waited for a question while he waited for me to agree with him.

"Yeah," I said finally.

"But she didn't call you."

"No."

He had lots of real questions I couldn't answer.

No, I didn't know where Darcy was supposed to be.

Did she have a job? Maybe.

Where did she usually stay? In her truck or sometimes with a friend. No, I didn't know who.

He sighed. "Do you have a photo of her?"

We were both relieved when I said yes. I texted him a picture of Darcy on her eighteenth birthday, a little more than a year ago. I'd taken her to dinner at a barbecue shack, just the two of us. She wore a lacy white low-cut blouse, her shortest miniskirt, and a walking cast on her right foot.

The photo was a good one. She wasn't posing or mugging, just smiling a little. It was easy to see her lean face and the thick rope of straw-yellow hair hanging over her shoulder. Her head was turned a little so the four-inch scar on her jaw wasn't visible.

The deputy said he'd send the photo around. If she didn't turn up in twenty-four hours, they'd put a search together. He thought the truck may have been there a day already, maybe two.

The post office sits at the end of town where the road changes from county pavement to one-lane gravel before disappearing into the Pisgah National Forest, half a million acres of wilderness. It's not really a town, more like a couple of buildings on a flood-prone riverbank between two mountains. Next to the post office is a gas-and-sandwiches store and, beyond that, a campground entrance with a trailhead into the forest.

On a busy summer weekend, hundreds of day-hikers and campers swarm into the Pisgah. Then the post office yard becomes an overflow parking lot. With all that traffic, no one gave Darcy's broken-down truck a second glance until the campground crowd cleared out early Monday.

I figured Darcy would turn up on her own in a day or two with an elaborate story about spending the weekend with someone she met in a bar.

But this morning—Tuesday—I got another call from the sheriff's office. They were organizing a search, headquartered at the campground, and I needed to show up.

School was starting in a week and I should've been finalizing orientation for my third-graders. But I set that aside and drove out, stopping briefly to drop off a bag of grain for Darcy's horse, Wiley, who lives at a half-abandoned farm on the way to the campground. I'd found him grazing by the side of the road, on the wrong side of the pasture fence—not the first time he'd gotten out—so I spent a few extra minutes putting him back where he belonged, in the field with the beef cattle and a lonely donkey.

By the time I arrived, the county's search-and-rescue team had rounded up a couple dozen volunteers. The parking lot was crowded with ATVs and big-wheel pickups, pre-coated with mud. Farmers and hunters wearing

Carhartt and camo clustered by the restrooms. They looked busy and important as they checked radios, shrugged into blaze-orange vests, and squinted at photocopied maps.

A deputy I'd never met, a restless, bulked-up cop named Jeffries in a tight khaki shirt and aviator shades, pulled me aside. Someone had seen a blond girl hitchhiking, he told me. Two days earlier, out on the county road.

"We're thinking it was Darcy. She must've set out on foot."

"I've been thinking about that," I told him. "I don't think she was on foot—"

"Yeah, she must've thumbed a ride with the wrong person."

"That's not what I meant. Her horse—"

"She's a pretty girl, right? We're not assuming foul play, not yet, but yeah." Jeffries nodded, agreeing with himself.

"That's not what I meant—"

Someone called "Deputy!" and he pivoted away. I leaned against my Jeep, wondering what I was supposed to do next.

Was Darcy pretty? I never thought so. All those scars, and way too skinny. But our mother always said I was the smart one and the responsible one, so where did that leave Darcy?

Jeffries came back and resumed his spiel. He talked about BOLOs and mapping apps, K-9 trackers and tri-state coordination. They were setting up a phone-in tipline. They'd find her, and the bastard that took her.

When he stopped for breath, I told him I'd seen Darcy's horse that morning, wandering outside his pasture. Not more than a half mile from here, by the side of the county road.

He shrugged it off. A loose horse, no big deal, happens all the time around here. Someone left the gate open or the horse jumped out.

"Yeah, but—" My jaw was starting to clench up. "Wiley—that's her horse—he was all sweated up. Like someone rode him this morning. Maybe Darcy went up one of the trails on horseback, into the Pisgah. Maybe we should be looking there."

His eyebrows climbed over the aviators. "You think your sister went for a ride on her horse, instead of looking for help after her truck broke down?" He aimed his gaze at the mountain behind me. "Was the horse wearing a saddle?"

"No, just a halter. With a short piece of rope."

"Well, there you are. A halter's what you use to lead a horse, not to ride a horse. Best thing is, you go home and wait someplace where you'll have a reliable phone signal. Call me if you hear anything."

He added a chin-jerk, indicating my Jeep.

I really wanted to grab Deputy Jeffries by his shirt and yell in his face but I decided that would be a bad idea.

Instead, I brought up my schoolteacher's voice. "A really good rider like my sister Darcy doesn't need a saddle. She rides bulls in rodeos, for chrissake."

But he was talking into his radio. I don't think he heard me.

***

"Now what, Wiley? You've been here before. So, which way?"

His ears flicked back at my voice, but he didn't step forward.

I hadn't been on a horse for years. They can feel it if you're nervous so I faked confidence. But Wiley was pretty chill. He stood patiently on the bank of Watson's Creek at the edge of the Pisgah Forest. Shaking his head occasionally at gnats and deerflies and waited for the boss—that was me—to decide where to go.

We'd ridden along a well-marked path from the gravel access road to a streamside picnic site where the trail forked. Turn left and you'd have a pleasant stroll along the shady stream back to the main entrance. Choose the right fork, and you'll be scrambling up an overgrown game trail that doesn't appear on any Forest Service map. It threads a path through a jumble of boulders the size of bucket loaders, then climbs almost straight up into deep wilderness.

I'd ridden that unmarked trail once about a decade ago when Darcy was nine and I was fourteen. Some older kids had told her about a waterfall at the top of the mountain, so of course she had to see it.

That had been a tough ride. She'd had Wiley for only about a month then and his steering, or hers, was still kind of sketchy. On the way down the mountain, my old pinto mare Dixie tripped over a rock and came up lame. I'd had to get off and walk her home, stumbling downhill through loose rocks and mudslides. We didn't get back until after dark and of course Mom blamed me.

So no, I didn't *want* to follow that old game path today. But I could see hoofprints in the mud by the creek. Two sets, the same size as Wiley's. One set of tracks pointed straight up that unmarked trail and a second set showed where the same horse had come back down.

Wiley snorted, blowing the gnats from his nose and startling me. He shook his whole body like an oversized hound slinging off swamp water, reminding me it was decision time.

I lifted the reins and nudged his belly with my heels. We ducked under a low-hanging hemlock branch and began climbing.

The trail was steep with lots of switchbacks and Wiley was demonstrating some serious mountain-climbing skills. He's the same age as Darcy, nineteen, which for a horse is getting on in years. But he's muscled up from working cattle in the feedlots. He's surefooted and clever, a tough old hill pony apparently born with all-wheel-drive.

It was hard work, though. An hour in, Wiley and I were both dripping with sweat. My thighs burned and my back ached and I was cursing Darcy's saddle, a dried-out chunk of leather designed for barrel racing, not backcountry riding.

Our daddy would've scolded her about letting the care of that saddle slide along with everything else. Darcy loves that old trophy saddle, it was the biggest award she ever won at a rodeo, but it needed treating with neatsfoot oil to soften it up.

The lettering stamped on its scuffed skirts proclaimed their victory, hers and Wiley's: Champion Barrels, Girls 12-13, Yancy County 2012. From back when she was still in school and crazier about horses than broke cowboys and bonecracking bulls.

When we reached an almost-level section of the trail, I stepped down so Wiley could catch his breath. I leaned against his steaming oak-brown shoulder and inhaled his hot-earth smell of horse.

That's a special aroma. It's fresh-baled hay and livestock shows, apple-picking and corn-planting. Watching a newborn calf stand on shaky legs to find its mama for the first time. All that rural-kid life that's supposed to make up for having parents who earned too little and fought too much.

Two months ago, Darcy told me she needed a new horse. Something younger than Wiley and better trained for ranch work like roping calves and chasing steers. What she claimed her job was now, or would be soon, because some ranch owner had said he'd hire her full-time if she had a good cowhorse. She was kinda vague on the name of the ranch and the owner.

"What about Wiley?" I asked. "If you get a new horse, where will he go?"

"I'll retire him to a nice family. He can have an easy life, teaching little kids to ride."

That sounded great but she never got the money together to buy a new horse and she never found Wiley a retirement home.

Truth? She's never earned enough to feed herself, let alone a horse. It was my summertime tutoring that paid for Wiley's hay and horseshoes. Since I was footing the bills for his keep, I could've ridden him anytime I wanted. But I never asked and Darcy never offered. We'd both learned to ride as kids but horses were Darcy's thing, not mine. I never thought a horse would help me get what I wanted, so I quit riding after eighth grade.

For me, it's always been eyes on a different prize. Grades and graduation, a steady job, a steady husband. Check, check, check. Ryan says I was born grown up. I'm so responsible, he says, I'm boring.

Except I was buying Wiley's oats on the sly and Ryan never knew. He thought my side gig was paying for yoga classes. I hate yoga.

Good old Wiley. When his breathing steadied, I hauled myself back into the saddle and we resumed climbing. Where a fallen pine tree blocked the way, I hung onto the saddle horn and gave Wiley his head so he could lurch and leap over. By then, I was giving equal time to prayers and curses, and wondering about how we were going to get down off this mountain before dark without falling off a cliff and breaking a leg.

If Darcy were here, she'd say breaking a leg's not the worst thing that can happen.

"Not the bull's fault," she'd explained when I collected her at the hospital discharge desk. "I came off him wrong."

"There's a right way?" I'd swallowed three ibuprofens on the way to the hospital because when I get that angry, my jaw clenches shut and I get horrible headaches. I was able to speak so the ibuprofen must've been working.

"Any way's the right way, as long as you stay on for the buzzer."

"And did you? Stay on for eight seconds?"

"Nah. Two and a half. He was a real twisty bastard. They named him Killdevil Hill. Like the hill you're gonna die on, right?"

She said it with reverence, like being a twisty bastard was a good thing.

Way worse than the broken leg, she reminded me, was what happened four years earlier when our fed-up momma locked our juiced-up daddy out of the house. Two days later, Mom put our sorry little farm on the market and told Darcy to pack, they were getting an apartment in town and moving in with Mom's new boyfriend Herb.

Daddy wasn't exactly a catch—he hung onto his truck-driving jobs just long enough to qualify for unemployment, then spent his cash on booze and hunting gear—but he was good to us girls. I never knew what our mother saw in Herb, a paunchy plumber with bad breath and bad teeth. He inhaled two packs a day and communicated mostly by grunting.

"Bets, what are we going to *do*?" Darcy wailed the night after she and Mom moved into Herb's apartment.

I knew exactly what I was going to do: finish college, marry Ryan, teach little kids. Avoid going home.

But Darcy was only fifteen, so she was stuck. She said she had three good things left in her life, Wiley and her trophy saddle and an old hunting knife that Daddy gave her. She said she'd left me, her big sister, off her good-things list because I'd abandoned her.

A couple of years later, Darcy told me she used to keep that knife stashed under her pillow at night because Herb always stood a little too close and gave her the creeps. My sister was silent about some things and a total drama queen about others so the knife and Herb's creepiness may or may not have been true.

Mom said it was a relief to live with a man who didn't get drunk every night and smash things. By "things" maybe she meant herself as well as the furniture. I never asked.

Darcy was a marginal student at best but her grades really went down the toilet after they moved. She was probably a little dyslexic but no one talked about it, and maybe social services should've gotten involved but no one called them. She quit school the day she turned sixteen.

Her first cowboy was a calf-roper, a soft-spoken Texan who taught her to roll a joint and drive a stick shift. He had a mattress in the back of his Silverado and a spare slot in his horse trailer. She and Wiley joined him on his tour of a bush-league rodeo circuit.

Then the Texas roper quit rodeos and got a job on a ranch in Montana so Darcy moved in with a bronc rider who convinced her to forget about the relatively safe sport of girls' barrel racing and learn how to chase bigger thrills, riding the roughstock. That's rodeo-speak for broncs and bulls, those violent, rider-hating animals that are bred and trained to explode into a bucking, pitching frenzy that hurls riders into the dirt.

Broncs, Darcy explained, bucked higher and came down harder than bulls, but the bulls were more challenging because they could spin and corkscrew in mid-air. And when a rider comes off a bucking horse, the bronc usually just gallops away. But a really mean bull might try to kill his rider. Darcy thought the bulls were more fun than the broncs.

After her first broken rib during a practice ride, bought her a padded body protector off eBay. When her face caught a horn that broke her jaw, I bought her a padded helmet with a chin guard and face cage

Our conversation a month ago followed the usual pattern.

"You're wearing the helmet, right? Every ride?"

"Yeah. Of course, don't worry."

I heard the eye roll over the phone. I knew she was lying.

I couldn't bear to watch her ride, but every Monday I searched for new photos. Competing in public, she wore the gear. But I also saw the Insta pics from her Friday night practice rides. In those, she was often bareheaded with yellow braids flying, her skinny unprotected body whipped sideways by whatever furious beast she'd chosen to ride.

"Come *on*, Bets!" she'd wheedle. "Can't you show a little family pride here? I'm not a buckle bunny, one of those arm-candy bimbos who'll sleep with any asshole. Any buckles, I win myself."

"You haven't won any buckles. You're hooked on painkillers and the prize money's shit. Especially for girls."

"Women. We got a league. And I need the oxies so I can keep riding."

"You'll be crippled before you get good enough to earn back your entry fees."

"There's a guy from Australia making a movie about it. About us, women riding roughstock."

"Yeah, right. What's his name? How much is he paying you?"

"I don't care about the money."

"So he's not paying you."

"You don't understand. It's all about the **bulls**. That rush I get from a ride? That's how I know I'm real."

I've never questioned being real. It's like we weren't from the same planet, much less the same parents.

A five-year difference in age is manageable if you're in a family where the parents do some reliable parenting. Then later, when you and your little sister are both grown, you can laugh about how she tagged along everywhere and tattled on you and stole your makeup. Then she'd apologize for that time when she was seven, remember? When she threw her mittens in the creek and hid for hours in the attic, and when Mom came home she blamed you for the lost mittens and your lost sister.

You have to keep looking for her, Mom said. No matter how long it takes.

If that was the two of you in a normal family, you'd be giggling together now and tickling each other and shouting, "Sisters forever!"

Ryan was no help. He disapproved of Darcy and everything about her, her sparkly rodeo shirts and her boots caked with cowshit. Her habit of showing up for dinner unannounced and leaving with all the leftovers plus a little cash for groceries.

What with dropping out of school and getting sloshed with cowboys twice her age and spending money she didn't have and getting herself busted up, he told me, she'd pretty much trashed her whole life at nineteen.

Ryan didn't mention drugs so maybe he didn't know about that.

He said I enabled Darcy. I said I was trying to guide her. He didn't care about guidance, he cared about our money that somehow got wasted on her rodeos. How could we save for a down payment on a house if I kept rescuing Darcy?

He insisted I cut her off.

Two weeks ago, I made that phone call. Hardest thing I ever did.

"Sorry, Darcy. I can't do this anymore. Get clean, get a job, find Wiley a home, like you said."

"It's Ryan, isn't it?" She whispered over the phone like we were all in the same room and he might hear. "You can't cut me off just because Ryan hates me."

"Quit riding bulls. Get yourself clean," I repeated. "Get a job and a place to stay. Like a normal person."

"You make it sound like I'm totally fucked up. And I have a job, at Beekman's"

"Part-time under the table, minimum wage if you're lucky. Shoveling cow shit and stacking hay bales. Half the time you can't even do that because you're on crutches. Grow up."

Silence, then a sniffle.

I sighed. "Have you talked to Mom?"

"She's ghosting me." Her voice caught. "Look, if you can't help me pay for Wiley, then that's it. He's yours."

"I don't want your horse, I want you to quit the bulls and get off the oxies. Call me when you get it together."

***

By the time Wiley carried me onto the last high ridge it was late afternoon. We'd climbed a thousand feet up to a small clearing near the top of the mountain, all gravel and boulders and scrubby bushes. A spring trickled out of a ledge, forming a narrow stream that cascaded three feet down into a shallow pool. Darcy's waterfall.

The air was cool and I had an awesome view of the mountains. At eye level, a pair of hawks rode a thermal. Far below, Watson's Creek wound along the valley floor to the distant campground. Beyond was the post office parking lot where Darcy's truck sat.

I climbed off and loosened Wiley's cinch while he drank from the pool. Then I tied his reins tight to a scrubby oak so he couldn't wander away without me.

I walked along the stream and around the edge of the ridgetop, seeing no sign that Darcy had been there. Had I ridden all that way for nothing?

At one side of the clearing, a mattress-sized ledge of granite overhung a sharp drop-off. I walked toward the edge but I've never liked heights so when I got close to the rim, I dropped down on hands and knees and eased forward between two boulders to peer over.

Then I scrambled back fast because there was nothing out there except air and dizziness. Step off that cliff and you'd drop a hundred feet straight down onto treetops and sharp rocks.

When I could breathe again, I stood and looked back to check on Wiley. He was dozing by the oak tree, one hind foot cocked and his tail swinging lazily.

And there, on a mossy boulder a few yards from the ledge, was a cellphone.

The case was filthy and the screen was cracked. I recognized it immediately, my sister's latest pay-as-you-go.

"Darcy?" My voice was first a whisper, then a whimper. "Darcy?"

Then I planted my feet wide on the gravel and bellowed, screaming her name over and over until the forest was shocked into silence and I had no sound left.

Nothing changed. The small stream rippled, Wiley dozed by his tree, and Darcy's phone sat on its bed of moss.

I pulled out my own phone and tried calling Deputy Jeffries. No signal.

A thought surfaced. What had I said to Darcy, the last time we spoke?

Call me when you get it together.

And then I remembered. She **had** called me, only twelve hours earlier. A little after four a.m., my phone began vibrating in its cradle on the nightstand while I, thick-headed with sleep, tried to work its buzz into a dream I was in the middle of.

It woke Ryan. He'd reached over me and shut it off before I knew what he was doing.

"Do *not* pick up," he'd hissed. "She'll leave a message. Go back to sleep."

I fell back into dreaming and when I woke for real at seven, I'd forgotten the call. She never left a message and she never called back.

Damn. *Damn.*

Some part of me saw that the sun was getting low. In the deepest coves, evening shadows were already creeping in. Wiley and I needed to get off this mountain and find help.

An eerie, flute-like whistle broke the quiet. Darcy's ringtone, the theme from *The Good, the Bad and the Ugly.* Her favorite movie.

Wiley's ears pricked and he turned his head.

Her phone had a different carrier but still, how could there be a signal up here?

The caller was someone named Jake. My hand hovered and the screen faded. I'd missed it. Or imagined it.

The screen flickered to life again with a voicemail alert.

I knew Darcy's password; I've always known her passwords. I touched the screen and found it. Heard a man's voice fading and rising against the white-noise background of a faraway crowd, or maybe road noise. Hard to understand, but I heard enough.

More footage, he said. The roughstock project, schedules, script approvals. Liked the backstory, needed more photos.

The voice cleared near the end. "Back in two days, with my mate."

I heard *dies* for days, *mite* for mate. The Australian moviemaker existed and his name was Jake.

The voice of Jake paused, waiting like me for Darcy to answer.

"Hey Darcy, you there?"

Silence.

The person in the clearing who seemed to be me—a vacant, distant me—sat on the mossy boulder for an unknown length of time. Eventually she remembered that they—she and Wiley, me and Wiley—needed to get down the mountain before dark. That person tightened Wiley's cinch and swung into the saddle.

With zero guidance from his rider, Darcy's horse slid and stumbled his way down to the valley just after sundown. Near the end of the ride, Wiley's rider found a cell signal and a voice and began making calls.

At the farm, I unsaddled Wiley. Hosed him off and fed him because that's what our Daddy taught us: You take care of your horse before yourself. I hugged Wiley around his warm, wet neck, because he'd been taking care of us all along.

At the campground, I located a different deputy, a pleasant-looking older woman who listened and asked good questions. I described the trail and showed her the photos I didn't remember taking. The clearing, the little waterfall, and Darcy's cell phone on the mossy boulder.

By then it was full-on dark and gone cloudy, threatening rain. The search would re-group at dawn, bringing in a tactical team with climbing gear and drones. They'd find her, the deputy assured me.

I went home. Said something forgettable to Ryan and waited.

***

It was five days with no news. This morning, the sheriff's office called to tell me they'd found a body on the east side of the mountain, half a mile downslope from the clearing. No ID yet, something about the remains being scattered.

I don't believe it's Darcy. Lots of people hike the backcountry in late summer. Until I know different, I'll stick with my routine.

School starts in three days and I've told the principal not to worry, I'll be there to greet my new third-graders. It's important to get them started off right.

Until then I'm spending an hour or two each morning with Wiley, out at the farm. Sometimes I sit on a hay bale and work on lesson plans but usually, I just brush my horse and pick the burrs out of his mane. I tell him things he might not know about my sister, from before he joined our family. How she loved to climb trees, going to the very top where the thin branches shivered. She'd want to go fishing for brim in the old quarry lake, but then she'd get bored and jump off the boat into the deepest coldest water and stay under until I was certain she'd drowned.

I believe I've worked it out, what happened to my sister.

She abandoned her broken-down truck before dawn and walked to the farm by the light of the setting moon. She fetched a halter and rope and climbed over the gate. Walked past the drowsy cattle and through the tall wet grass, soaking her boots with dew. She called softly so Wiley wouldn't be startled up from where slept in the lower pasture by the river. She swung a leg over his strong bare back, wrapped her calves around his ribs, and wound her fingers in his mane. They rode to the trailhead just as dawn broke with mist rising from the fields, whispering around them like a living thing.

What else was there for her to do then but gallop along the creek? What else but follow the ancient game trails, climb the mountain, and find her waterfall?

I tell myself that even if I'd remembered to call her back that morning, it wouldn't have changed a thing. By the time I was making coffee, she'd already set her cell phone on that rock by the little pool.

Maybe she tripped and hit her head and forgot where she left her phone. Maybe Wiley wandered off and she tried to follow him but lost the trail. Or she simply set him free, sending him back down the mountain to find me.

It's all a terrible mistake. I think she'll just show up one day, maybe with a new limp and more bruises.

She'll laugh and flip back that rope of yellow hair. Then she'll say she'd like her phone back, please. And her horse, and me.

An excerpt from the author's new novel, *A Knowledge of Darkness* (release: Autumn 2026)

A KNOWLEDGE OF DARKNESS

April 20

St. Johnsbury, Vermont

Just before the first bullet hit him, Jonathan Wilder was harvesting lettuce.

The sun had just dropped behind the Green Mountains, and long shadows slanted across the raised beds as daylight eased into a soft dusk. Evenings like this were exactly why he'd bought this old hill farm.

His garden was productive, despite the hard ground and long winters. He was pleased that his wife Maya had suggested a fresh salad with dinner, wanting to celebrate the spring that had taken so long to arrive.

Wilder moved along the rows with his new garden shears. Secateurs, the garden shop clerk had called them. Made of Japanese steel, able to lop off a one-inch branch. Definitely overkill for snipping baby spinach, but Wilder liked the feel of the small powerful tool in his hand.

Their three Highland cows grazed in the far pasture, darker shapes against the steep slope of Moosekill Knob. One of the heifers lowed once, the sound carrying beneath the shrill, insistent songs of spring peepers and wood frogs in the pond below the garden. He heard Maya calling the chickens into the coop behind the barn, scolding the stragglers.

After twenty minutes crouched over the beds, Judge Wilder straightened to his full six-three height and stretched his back. Sixty-six years old, and his body still carried every injury: the knee shattered in Fallujah, the shoulder that never healed right after the Humvee rollover, ribs that ached before every weather change. He'd learned to read these old signals the way he read case files, paying close attention as he pieced together evidence.

The cows stopped grazing and lifted their heads, staring toward the dark woods beyond their pasture.

Wilder set down his basket and turned to follow their gaze, shears still in his left hand. To the south, the steep slope of the Knob loomed dark and familiar in the twilight, the same as always. In the east, a bright planet had risen — Saturn, he thought; his daughter Morgan would certainly know.

Turning back toward the woods, he looked for the familiar shape of a deer or turkey, but night had crept close while he was thinking of dinner and it was too dark now to see into the trees.

There was no movement, but the frogs had gone quiet and the quality of the stillness had changed. He'd felt this before, in places where abrupt silence meant danger..

It could be a coyote or a bobcat, a common predator hoping to find the henhouse door still open. One hand moved toward his hip before he remembered he wasn't carrying. All he had was garden shears, a basket of lettuces, and thirty years of muscle memory telling him when something wasn't quite right.

A human figure walked up from the fence by the lower field and Jonathan relaxed. Not coyotes on the hunt, just a hiker stumbling downhill through the dusk on the way home after climbing the Knob. The public trail ran through the woods just above their cow pasture, and walkers sometimes got lost coming down in the fading light. Out too late, getting cold, looking for a shortcut back to town.

"Hello," the judge called. "Have you lost the trail? The road's right over there if you want to follow it back. Just walk down our driveway." He waved his free hand toward the white mailbox, a hundred yards away and barely visible in the gloom.

The walker came closer, but not near enough for him to make out the face. In the left hand, a flashlight? But there was no beam of light. He—or she, hard to tell—wore dark clothing and a knitted watch cap pulled low. A wise choices for the cool spring evening.

The person stopped about twenty feet away and raised the flashlight.

No, not a flashlight. The judge frowned and tightened his grip on the shears. "What is this about—"

The first shot took him high in the right shoulder, shattering his collarbone and spinning him sideways. He dropped the secateurs and clapped his left hand over the wound.

There'd been no loud bang, just a muted thud. His brain tried to process caliber, trajectory, distance—but the information wouldn't resolve.

They're using a suppressor, he had time to think. *That's good, Maya won't hear it, she's still in the barn. But I have to warn her—*

The second shot caught him below the ribs, punching through and exiting near his spine. His legs stopped working and he went down hard among the spinach, crushing plants he'd been nurturing for weeks.

The sky had blackened and stars were beginning to show. The judge tried to turn his head toward the figure, to identify something, but his neck wouldn't cooperate.

His breath came in ragged wet gasps. Dimly aware of footsteps approaching, he tried to speak—to ask *who*, or maybe *why*—but only blood came.

He knew this day might come, but he always thought he'd have a little more time.

Someone moved into his narrowing field of vision and crouched close. The face was in shadow and Jonathan was only vaguely aware of boots, black gloves, a handgun held with casual competence.

"Been waiting a good long while for this, Judge." The words were said lightly but carried a deep satisfaction. "And jeez, it feels good."

The voice was almost familiar. The judge's mind reached for connections, for which case, which defendant, which conviction had brought them together here—but the effort felt enormous. He thought he had it, he almost had it—but the answers scattered.

The third shot entered his temple and the stars went out.

***

The hard twist of tension in the shooter's throat began to ease. *So far, so good.* He slipped off a small backpack, unscrewed the suppressor, and tucked the handgun away.

He started to pull a hunting knife from a side pocket, but saw the secateurs lying at the judge's feet, practically begging to be used for something more challenging than spinach.

The curved shears fit perfectly when placed just below the middle knuckle of the judge's right pinky. One quick squeeze was all it took and the bloody token went into a plastic bag.

He held the shears for a moment longer, being tempted. Thinking, *they're new, expensive, very useful*, and also *wages of sin, a small compensation*. But then the words *discipline* and *purpose* and *caution!* floated to the surface of his brain. Moving to the far side of the judge's body, he placed the shears carefully in the slack left hand and fold dead fingers over the handles.

It was a silly, impulsive gesture, but it seemed right somehow. Almost noble. *He died in his garden. Let the man hold his tools.*

Selecting next a small flashlight, flicking it on but keeping it cupped in his hand, the killer retraced his steps and began searching for bullet casings.

A phone rang faintly. The killer froze, staring at the dark bulk of the farmhouse thirty yards away. A light had come on inside, shining through the pale curtains of a single window.

The phone stopped mid-ring and silence fell. A single wood frog resumed its call, and a few others took up the chorus. The smell of disturbed earth and broken stems mixed with the metallic scent of blood.

The light from the house cast a faint glow across the yard. Just beyond the woven wire fence, the three cows stared blankly with heads lowered and tails twitching. Just cows, he knew. No bulls, so no danger there. And no dogs to raise an alarm, not since the judge's noisy little terrier had died over the winter.

He picked up the last shell and climbed awkwardly over the sagging wire into the pasture, scattering the cows. They lurched away into the dark and the night was quiet again.

Far enough away now, seeing no other night-walkers, he began a nearly soundless underbreath whistling that matched his stride and eased the last of the tension in his chest. The beam of his flashlight beam bobbed across the field, weaving around stones and thistles.

At the far fenceline, where pasture turned to forest, he climbed out over the wire mesh and found the hiking trail. Stopping only once, briefly, to look back.

More lights had come on in the Wilders' yard and house, framing the scene like a distant diorama. Even from hundreds of yards away, the judge's body was visible among the dark shadows of the raised beds. One arm flung wide and the other by his side, reaching for a weapon that wasn't there.

The killer swung the flashlight back to the well-worn path and quickened pace. Where the trail forked, choosing the uphill track and heading away from town. It would be twenty minutes more to the other side of the Knob, near the St. Johnsbury entrance ramp for I-91.

The climb grew steeper. The whistling was replaced by quicker breaths and random thoughts about how other people always said Wilder had been such a fair judge.

Serving the course of justice, balancing compassion with a desire to keep the community safe, blah blah blah.

Other people say a lot of stupid shit. This is justice.

Acknowledgments

Here's where I pay homage to the tenets I follow:
Keep writing. You can *always* make it better.
Don't kill your darlings; find them a new home.
Embrace your writing community.

These thirteen stories have been written over a span of four decades—and at least two of them have been in revision during most of that time.

The first draft of the oldest, "Not a Burden," was written in the early 1990s. It found early success, winning the 1993 Dorothy Daniels Award from the National League of American Pen Women, but wasn't actually published until 2025, when it found a home in the Association of Rhode Authors' 2025 anthology (and earned a Pushcart Prize nomination).

"Witnessing"—perhaps my favorite—is nearly as old, and it wins the award for the most revisions. In an earlier iteration, it earned an award from the Asheville Writers' Workshop, but then went through several rejections—and extensive rewriting—before also finding a home in 2025.

In all my writing, I want to explore the geographies and cultures that shape our everyday lives. Each setting becomes a character in its own right: a farm in Hawai'i, a remote mountain top in North Carolina, an old mill town in New England.

With all the years and experiences that go into my writing, I want to acknowledge those who have helped me along the way.

First, a big thank you to my current writers' groups, hosted at Booklovers Gourmet bookshop in Webster, Massachusetts, and the Putnam Library writers' group in Putnam, Connecticut. Thank you especially to early readers (and talented writers) Brynn Turner, Jess Andersen, Karen Warinsky, Jason Richards, and Corlis Fraga.

Several earlier stories were read, critiqued, and given enthusiastic support by the Weaverville Writers' Workshop in Weavervhille, North Carolina, and—going way back!—the Wolf Den Writers' Group in Pomfret, Connecticut.

None of this would be possible without the constant support of Rich Valcourt, my husband and best grammar grinch, who is always ready to celebrate every success or argue the necessity of an Oxford comma. Thank you for all you do, from the bottom of my heart.

All these stories have been previously published. Thank you to the many publications that have given these works a home, a voice, and an audience. Here's to all the editors of small and independent presses, working hard to find and showcase the important stories.

A New England farmer at heart, Sarah P. Blanchard has also lived in Hawai'i and North Carolina. Rural life and the natural world are always strong influences in her writing, as are the works of writers Barbara Kingsolver, Percival Everett, and Joyce Carol Oates.

Sarah holds a B.A. in English literature and an M.B.A. in marketing. She worked for many years in communications and marketing. On side journeys, she has been a volunteer firefighter, radio news anchor and talk show host, magazine editor, website developer, horse trainer, and facilities supervisor for Gemini Observatory. She taught English and communications for several years at the University of Hawaii-Hilo and also taught fiction writing in the College for Seniors Program in the Osher Lifelong Learning Institute at the University of North Carolina-Asheville.

In her writing, Sarah is drawn toward flawed, compassionate characters who believe they must battle their demons alone; and complex antagonists who think they have nothing to lose.

Also by Sarah P. Blanchard:

Fiction

Grabtown (novel, 2025; English and Spanish editions)
Drawn from Life (novel, 2024)
Playing Chess with Bulls (essay, short stories, 2023)

Poetry

river, horse, morning (2024)

Non-fiction

Jump with Joy (2007)
The Power of Positive Horse Training (2003)
Carriage Driving (with Heike Bean, 1993, 2004)

Follow the author

Website: sarahpblanchard.com
Facebook: @Sarah.P.Blanchard.author
Instagram and Threads: @sarahpblanchard
Tiktok: @sarah_p_b_author
Bluesky: @sarahpblanchard.bsky.social